DEATH IN ROOM 7

First published in Australia by South Coast Publishing, July 2015.
Copyright K.J. Emrick (2015)

This is a work of fiction. The characters, incidents and locations portrayed in this book and the names herein are fictitious. Any similarity to or identification with the locations, names, characters or history of any person, product or entity is entirely coincidental and unintentional.

- From a *Declaration of Principles* jointly adopted by a Committee of the American Bar Association and a Committee of Publishers and Associations.

All rights reserved. No part of this publication may be reproduced or transmitted in any form or by any means, electronic or mechanical, including photocopy, recording, or any information storage or retrieval system, without permission in writing from the publisher.

No responsibility or liability is assumed by the Publisher for any injury, damage or financial loss sustained to persons or property from the use of this information, personal or otherwise, either directly or indirectly. While every effort has been made to ensure reliability and accuracy of the information within, all liability, negligence or otherwise, from any use, misuse or abuse of the operation of any methods, strategies, instructions or ideas contained in the material herein, is the sole responsibility of the reader. Any copyrights not held by publisher are owned by their respective authors.

All information is generalized, presented for informational purposes only and presented "as is" without warranty or guarantee of any kind.

All trademarks and brands referred to in this book are for illustrative purposes only, are the property of their respective owners and not affiliated with this publication in any way. Any trademarks are being used without permission, and the publication of the trademark is not authorized by, associated with or sponsored by the trademark owner.

ISBN: 1515353117
ISBN-13: 9781515353119

DEATH IN ROOM 7

K J EMRICK

CHAPTER ONE

I think what I like most about Lakeshore, is how peaceful it is.

A sleepy little community in the southern tip of Tasmania, settled among the pines, nestled at the edge of three lakes that feed into each other and help keep the climate mild and cool. The breeze off those lakes is right nice. I like the way it smells. It reminds me of my childhood, as a little girl growing up in Sydney, with the ocean at my doorstep. These lakes here aren't the ocean, but they're great just the same.

We've got fine folks who live here, too. Make a living off the tourists who come to spend some time here in the foothills of the Hartz Mountains. Get people in from all over the world. Even as far away as America and Canada. Nice to meet new friends. 'Course, I run the only Inn here in town. The Pine Lake Inn. Put it right on the water. Open year round. A quiet place, in a quiet town.

Until something happens.

Today started like any other day for me and Rosie. She'd cooked up some amazing Jumbuck stew to serve the guests for lunch. Rosie's good that way. That's why she runs the kitchen side of the Inn and I run the business side. Ever since University, it's been our dream to own our own Inn. Now we do. Doing a good bit of business for ourselves, too. That's saying something in this economy.

So life was going on as usual, with the lunch made and the reservations set for the next few days, and George the handyman even managing to fix that leaky faucet in room four. The Pine Lake Inn's got three floors, two for guest rooms and then the bottom floor for the dining room and the commons area. We have rooms for fifteen boarders, then there's my room at the end of the third floor. One of the perks of being the owner.

Rosie's got her own place in town. She and that husband of hers need the privacy. Trying to make a family, they are. Been trying for a long time. Not something that happens overnight.

"I'm telling you," Rosie was saying to me, "it's not for lack of trying. Poor Josh. I wear the poor man out almost every night."

"Rosie!" I laugh, hooking a strand of my long hair behind my ear, feeling my cheeks heat up even though we've had this talk more than once. That's how close we are. Best friends forever, is how the kids say it nowadays. 'Course, I haven't been a kid for a while now. Can't hardly see twenty in the rearview, as they say. Forty-three was the birthday I celebrated last.

Been a good life so far. Had my ups and downs, but then doesn't everyone?

We're setting tables in the dining room at the moment. Lunch hasn't started yet. We begin serving guests at eleven o'clock for lunch, and it's only half past ten now. Rosie is always happy to make something for the guests at any hour, but the brochure says eleven so most people don't come down from their rooms til close to that time. Gives me and her a little time to ourselves to talk about the state of affairs in Australia in general and our own lives, too.

"You think maybe my Mister would be more into it if I lost me a few pounds?" Rosie asks me. She stood up straight in her dark slacks and her short white chef's coat, and runs her hands down her plump form.

I think Rosie looks just fine the way she is. She's a real woman, not one of those airbrushed models in the mags. She's the same age

I am, with to-die-for brown eyes and hair to match, an oval face with a cute little mouth and a beauty mark on her left cheek. Any man hereabouts would be lucky to have her as a wife. She's always smiling and happy. I know for a fact that her Josh can't get enough of her.

Kind of like my ex-husband had been with me.

Clearing my throat to disperse sad memories, I wink at Rosie. "You're great, Rosie. Men have fought wars over women like you. I wouldn't worry about making Josh more interested in you. Just show up tonight with a bottle of wine. Clothes optional."

"Oh, go on with ya." It was Rosie's turn to twitter with laughter, and I could hear her humming away as we worked after that.

The kitchen is just off the main foyer, where the registration desk stands with the phone and computer and sign-in book. It's a little old school, but I like to have people actually sign their names when they check in. I could hear the phone out there starting to ring just as we finished setting plates out on the last table. They're the new ones I bought with the floral pattern to match the wallpaper. They look great, I think, but for now I'm sure Rosie can handle the rest of the setting up. I step out to the desk to answer the phone.

"If that's our ghost, tell him I say hello!" Rosie calls after me.

The "ghost" is our running joke. Sometimes the phone rings and there's no one there. Things like that happen everywhere, but here more than most places. Had us a guest a few months back who thought maybe it was something more than just phone troubles. Miss Darcy Sweet sure did stir up an interesting time in our sleepy little town, but now things were back to normal, and a phone was just a phone.

I pick up the gray receiver on the sixth ring, just before it would have gone to voicemail. "G'day, Pine Lake Inn. How can I help you?"

There was a short pause before the person on the other end of the line said anything. "Dell? Is that you? It's me, Jessica."

I remember that voice. "Jessica? Jessica Riley? Lord have mercy, I sure wasn't expecting to hear from you. How are you?"

"Starving, actually. It's a bugger of a long drive from Hobart. Am I even on the right road?"

Was she even on the right…? Oh! "Are you coming here?"

"Sure am. In fact, I'm only thirty minutes away from ya. I think. GPS is on the fritz. I got off at Geeveston onto Huon but this is a blooming donkey track!"

I laugh at her. "That's the road. The only road, as a matter of fact. Follow it in. The streets in town are paved, I promise. Where are you staying?"

Her voice turned to static for a moment before it cleared again. "…not like the old days. Don't know as many blokes there in town like I used to."

"Are you on your mobile while you're driving? Pull over, girl! You keep dropping out."

"Now, Dell, I'd never do something illegal. This is me."

I could hear the smile in her voice. Back in university with me and Rosie, Jessica was always a bit of a hellraiser. She'd gotten suspended from the dorms at one point. Had every guy chasing after her, too. Nobody'd ever accuse her of being a straight arrow. "Don't give it a thought, Jess. You'll stay here. We've got a few empty rooms. My treat."

"Dell, I couldn't…"

The line went static again, and I waited.

In the static I was sure I heard a man's voice, whispering something, but I couldn't make out what.

It couldn't be, of course.

"Ya there?" Jess asked, suddenly loud and clear.

"Er, yeah. Sure am. You have someone with you?"

"No, just me. Why?"

Huh. "Sorry, musta been the white noise. Your call dropped for a bit."

"I was saying I couldn't let ya give me a room without paying. Won't hear of it. I've got me enough cash packed away to choke a horse. Book me a room, but I'll be paying my bill."

I rolled my eyes. There was no arguing with Jess when her mind was made up. Once she set her heart on something, she made a straight line for it and never turned left or right. "Okay, Jess. We'll set you up in a room. Come straight here when you're in. All right?"

Once I gave her the directions, we said our goodbyes and hung up. Excitement mixed with other emotions inside of my brain. It had been years since me and Jess had seen each other, and I knew I'd changed. A lot can happen to people in a lifetime. She sounded like she'd been successful, insisting on paying for the room, talking about how much money she had, and all that. Jess had always landed on her feet no matter how much trouble she got into.

Then there was me, and Rosie, and our Inn. Looking around me now, I see the dark wood paneling and the hardwood floors, the handwoven throw rugs, the little fireplace over in the corner. I see the pictures framed on the walls showing beautiful scenes of the area around Lakeshore, or landmarks from all over Australia like Sydney's Opera House and the Uluru monolith. Every wall has something to show, except for that one space on the corner leading to the kitchen where nothing will hang. Ever.

I can't see the commons area from here, but I have it memorized by heart. Tall windows, a warm and inviting space filled with overstuffed chairs and a television and books and games for guests to play. The dining room and kitchens are on the other side of the bottom floor. Above me are the guest rooms, each one unique and tidy and perfect.

This is my Inn. Mine, and Rosie's. I may not be wildly successful and rich, but I'm proud of the place. We created something special. No reason to be disappointed in what we've done here.

Maybe it was myself I was disappointed in, I wondered, not realizing I was feeling that little bit of jealousy until I'd heard my own thoughts. There's a mirror over on the wall, left of the entrance to the commons area. It's an ornate thing with a crafted frame. In its reflection, I see my face.

It's not an old face, no matter how old I feel some days. The freckles across the bridge of my nose and my cheeks will always keep me looking young. So does the deep auburn hair that spills down over my shoulders. The purple top I wear is tight in all the right places, and my wide black belt accentuates slim hips and a stomach I have to work to keep flat, nowadays. I've heard my body compared to a twenty-year old's, and I'll take that compliment. My husband used to tell me that, and other things too, in the middle of the night…

Ahem. Hubby's gone now, of course. Gone in a puff of smoke to points unknown. Gone four years last week, as a matter of fact. On my birthday. Never came back. Got one of those uncontested divorces for Christmas last year, and what else could I do? Sad as that makes me, I remember the good times with him, and I move on.

One of my clear green eyes winks back at me. "Don't matter what other people think. You're beautiful, Adelle Powers. Simply beautiful."

Finally, I smile, knowing that I'm being foolish anyway. Jessica is a friend. No matter how successful she's become, she wouldn't hold it against me even if I was broke and ugly. Which I'm not. So.

Whistling a tune, I head back into the kitchen to let Rosie know that Jess is coming. She'll be happy to hear it, if for no other reason than it means one more meal to prepare in her kitchen.

On the way to the kitchen a shadow passes down the stairs. Shadows don't usually move. Stopping quick enough that my black sneakers squeak against the floorboards, I turn, and see the shadow standing still, watching me.

Oh, snap.

Mister Brewster smiles at me, but as usual his smile doesn't touch his eyes. He's a tall man, and dark, which explains why he looked like a moving shadow from the corner of my eye, I suppose. Dark hair cut short and shaggy around a lean and angularly shaped head. Dark shirt with a high collar. Dark pants and boots. Dark, almost black eyes. As a guest, he's the dream of everyone who ever owned an Inn. He pays his bill in advance, keeps his room tidy, doesn't disturb anyone, and hardly ever comes out of his room.

He's just so damn creepy.

Not that I'd ever hold that against the man. Or anyone for that matter. We live in a town at the edges of civilization here in Tasmania. Tassie, as a lot of the locals call her. Lots of oddballs out here. Good, dear folks like Mrs. Havernathy with her jams or crazy Arthur Loren digging for gold in the dust. Lots of characters in this town.

What's one more?

Mister Brewster walks by, and I wait for him to seat himself at one of the few empty tables in the dining room before I go through to the kitchen to find Rosie. He always orders the same thing. Figure I can tell Rosie to get it ready for him now. Right after I give her the good news about Jessica's visit.

The place had filled up in the length of time I was on that phone call. Nice to see the servers rushing back and forth to keep up with the orders.

We redid the kitchen a few months back. The backsplash is now this gorgeous white and pink tile motif behind a brand new double stove that includes a wood burning oven on the side. Cupboards of deep, dark wood. Rosie ran a neat and tidy kitchen, every spice in its place and every pan hung on its proper hook. It was odd, when you considered how accident prone she was. I almost expect everything to be topsy turvy each time I step in here. If there was anyone who could benefit from a universal health care system in Australia, it would be Rosie Ryan.

Right now she's hard at work getting the menu ready for dinner. Lunch hasn't even started yet, but there was bread that needed to be put in the oven and meats spiced and prepared and a whole lot of other things that I'm just as happy to leave for my partner to take care of. The cooking part of things was never my strongpoint. I'm great with the finances, but to make a run at it the Inn needs more than ace paperwork. It needs Rosie's creative flair in the kitchen.

I found her right where I expect her to be, peering into one of the oven doors at whatever was baking there.

"Hey, Rosie," I say when she closes the oven. I didn't want her to spook and catch her hair on fire.

Yes, that's happened before. Only the one time.

"What d'ya say, Dell?" she answers me with a big smile, wiping her hands on the apron. "Got a few customers in today for lunch, didn't we?"

"Do you have enough jumbuck stew to go around?"

As servers rushed in and out of the room, bringing the plates and bowls of prepared food out to the guests and locals who came in for a good meal, Rosie lifted the lid of a tall, metal pot, and the aroma of thick gravy simmering with vegetables and tender meat fills the room. "Sure do. Everybody likes the stew."

"I know someone who doesn't."

Rosie's face soured. "He's down for lunch, then, is he?"

Death in Room 7

"Yes. Mister Brewster came in just before me. I imagine he'll want his usual steak sandwich, done rare and tender. Might as well make it now, right?"

"Hmph," she scoffs, crossing her arms over her full chest. "Rare and tender. More like bloody and raw. Ah well. No accounting, I suppose. I'll do it up for him."

"Thanks. I actually came back here to tell you something really awesome. You'll never guess who that was on the phone."

When I tell her about Jess, about her coming here to Lakeshore, the response I get is a lot less enthusiastic than I had expected.

"Oh." With that single word, Rosie busies herself with sprinkling flour over a raw lump of dough and then kneading it with her hands.

"That's all?" I ask, knowing that I'm missing something. "Just, oh? You don't have anything else to say about it?"

Rosie shrugged. "That's nice, I guess." She hits the lump of dough a little harder than she really needs to. "No, actually, I don't think that's nice. I know she was your mate back in Uni and all, Dell, but Jessica was always trouble. Getting into something she shouldn't, and then not caring who she dragged along with her."

I stand there, a little stunned, not sure how to respond to that. I never knew that Rosie felt like that about Jess. "We were all friends back then, remember?"

She took down cinnamon and a few other spices, and took her time seasoning the dough before she said anything else. "You and Jess was great pals. You and me were the best of friends, always will be. But me and Jess? Not so much. She's trouble, that one. Just don't want her bringing it here."

"Oh, Rosie. I'm sure it's not like that. You'll see."

My friend nodded, and smiled, but it wouldn't take much to see she wasn't convinced. Well. I can't really argue with her. Jess made her own reputation, with no help from anyone else, but she was always a good person in her heart. Whatever Rosie remembered from back in our University days, I knew my friend wasn't coming here to cause trouble. Rosie might need some convincing, but I knew Jessica's visit was going to be just great.

The server's rushed in and out again, black vests and white shirts pressed and perfect. I hired people from Geeveston and other local towns for the busier times of the season and right now, I was in their way. I've had to lay them off a few times when things slowed down and there weren't that many guests to take care of, but for the most part the Pine Lake Inn is always a busy place.

I left them to it and went to check a few things in the registration book. Everything is on the computer, too, but there's something very intimate in letting people write their names and information down for themselves. Makes them feel like friends. It's good business. It's neighborly, too.

After finishing up a few little tasks I start upstairs to my room. I've something I want to find up there. Before my husband left me we had a place of our own out in Lakeshore, out near the edge of town where the Monteray pine trees grow tall and thick and on a clear day we could see the tips of the Hartz Mountains. Sold that house over two years ago. No need for me to live in a big place like that anymore. Too many memories chasing around the corners.

The stairs from the second to the third floor are on the opposite end of the hallway from the first floor stairs. I check the rooms as I go, taking a look-see into the ones that aren't currently rented, just to be sure the cleaning lady I hired three weeks back is doing her job correctly. I've fired bludgers before who thought they could collect a paycheck and never sweep a floor. From what I can see, I've found me a good one. Every bed made up tight, everything in its place. Huh. Will wonders never cease?

DEATH IN ROOM 7

Up the stairs to the third floor, my mind started to wander back to Uni and all the times that Jess and me and Rosie would stay out late in a pub or catch a movie or get in trouble together. Now that I thought back on it, I do remember more than once when Rosie would beg off from our activities with a simple excuse of having to study or of being tired. Strange I never noticed it before. Well. We'll just have to show Rosie that Jess is a good person, deep down where it counts.

In the middle of that thought, the skin at the back of my neck crawled.

Have you ever had the feeling you were being watched? It happens to me, well, more often than it probably should. Especially here in my Inn. Things happen here that I can't explain. It's not just the way the phone will ring at odd times with no one on the other end of the line. Sometimes I'll set down a cup or a book just to turn away for a minute. When I turn back, things have been moved. The book is closed or the cup is out of reach or my nice, neat pile of paperwork is all out of order. I can see shadows moving that shouldn't move.

And I'm not talking about Mister Brewster.

Then there's moments like this, when I can feel a man's eyes on me, even though no one else is with me on the stairs.

I look up, then back down the way I just came. I really am alone. There's no one else here. That's a fact that my brain can accept, having seen the evidence with my own two eyes.

Still, my heart is racing and my skin is all goose pimply and my hand is gripping the banister tight enough for my knuckles to be white. My brain might know I'm alone, but the rest of me isn't buying it.

Do you believe in ghosts? I do. Never seen one myself but I believe they're just as real as the dingos that howl at night out in the Never-Never. So I have to wonder, when things are moved with no good explanation, or when every picture we hang on that one wall in the entryway falls crashing to the floor...are there ghosts in my Inn?

Or am I just bonkers?

That thought lets me smile at myself, even chuckle a little, and start up the stairs again. Bonkers it is. Every place has its own little quirks. Been in hotels where the pipes creaked all night and the television kept going on the fritz. Didn't mean it was ghosts. The Pine Lake Inn was like that. It had character. It had its own special ambience. It had a soul, after a fashion, but a soul isn't a ghost.

Even so, I make sure to shut the door to my room behind me and lock all three locks.

My room is a bit grander than most of the others in the Inn. Maybe not as big as room number nine, the Honeymoon Suite, but bigger than the single rooms to be sure. Arranged differently, too, since I lived here permanent like. I had a real closet built into the far wall, to the right of the tall window that looked out on the smooth surface of Pine Lake. There were a lot of little things I added after me and Rosie took it over. My bed wasn't all that big, but it was another personal touch I had brought into this room when I took it over. It has wooden banisters and a canopy with pink ruffles. I painted the walls in the same color with a white trim.

Hey, I like pink. I'm still a girly girl. When I want to be.

The ensuite bathroom is decorated in seashells. Shells on the wallpaper. A sink shaped like a scalloped shell. Even bottles holding tiny shells I've picked up along the coastline. My shower curtain is transparent except for very strategically placed sea shells. Just the two rooms, bedroom and bathroom, but I've managed to make them my own.

The entertainment stand to the left of the bathroom door held my television and DVD player and a stereo system that I never actually used because I didn't want to disturb the guests. It also held a row of paperback novels by different authors. Had my photo albums, too, and one other book that I hadn't looked through in years.

Opening the magnetic catch of the glass door, I slid out the tall book with its stiff blue cover. The name of my old University was scripted across the front, above a picture of the main building, and the year I graduated. A few more years back than I care to admit. Heh. Time moves on.

My yearbook creaked when I opened it. That's how long it's been since I've looked through it. The inside cover was filled with the names and well wishes and really bad limericks signed by the friends I'd had there. I found what Jess had written easily enough. Strong, blocky letters read, "Drink often, laugh more, and love with abandon."

I can't help but smile at that. Those words were Jess to a tee. Always living her life to the fullest, not worrying about what tomorrow might bring. It would be great to see her again.

Flipping through the pages, past the faces of people I'd forgotten all about, past a few others I promised myself to catch up with—someday—I find the photo of Jess. Thin, in that athletic way that men found so attractive. Long, honey-colored hair. Eyes that were always smiling even when the rest of her face was scowling. In the picture she looked like she was thinking about what mischief to cause next. Or, maybe that was just my mind adding details that weren't there.

Flipping to another page I find a photo of Jess and me mugging for the camera in the hallway of one of the buildings on campus. Dewey Hall? Druthers? I can't remember now. Not that it really matters. What matters is that we were happy back then. We had our whole lives ahead of us.

Well, life was happening around me now. I was happy, to be sure, but I wouldn't mind finding some of that carefree attitude

I could see in that photo of my younger self. I snapped the book closed and set it, face up, on the corner of my bed while I went into the bathroom to freshen up. Little water on my face. Reapply my mascara. Things like that. Jess was coming, and it was going to be grand. I couldn't wait to see her.

Blinking my eyes at myself in the mirror, I pursed my lips in a kiss, then laughed at myself. Just knowing Jess was coming had me feeling younger already.

Stepping back out into my bedroom I reached for the yearbook. And stopped.

It was now lying face down.

CHAPTER TWO

Bang, bang, bang.

"George, I've told you to just let it go."

I have, too. He's tried to hang that painting on the wall near the fireplace so many times I've lost track. Won't give up, though. Our handyman is nothing if not tenacious.

I think that's a Tassie word for just plain stubborn.

On top of his ladder, George flashes me a confident smile. "I know ya think it's a lost cause, Dell, but this painting of the honored Lieutenant Governor David Collins should hang in a good spot."

"Maybe so, George, but there's folks who would say old David Collins should just hang."

George gave me a look that said he didn't think my comment was funny. Politics in Australia is pretty serious for some. So's our history.

"Okay, George. What's the plan to get David Collins on our wall this time?"

Balancing on the ladder with his feet planted and his hips braced on the top step, George smiles at me and holds up a long hook with a threaded end like a screw. "These little buggers expand as ya screw 'em. Can't come out. Guaranteed."

"George! You've already put more'n a dozen holes in that wall already."

"I patched them all!" he protested, with a sideways glance at the wall beside him. "Well. Most all of 'em."

The painting of David Collins is perched on the top of the stepladder, and from his pale face with its dark eyebrows, the man's eyes seem to beg me for help. See? Even the painting knows it isn't going to work.

But George wants to try, so… "Have at it, George."

He winks one pale brown eye at me and runs a hand through his gray hair while he surveys the wall to find the perfect spot for his special, expanding screw hooks. Hopefully not somewhere he's already nailed or screwed or drilled. Yes, drilled, and don't think I didn't have a long talk with him after that little escapade. I'll give him this much. He doesn't give up.

He was still rapping the back of his knuckles against the wall when the door opened a few minutes later, and Jess came waltzing in.

George stopped what he was doing, knuckles in the air, to stare. Couldn't blame him. She looked exactly like she had in University. Like there hadn't been a dozen—or so—years between then and now. Slim, feminine curves under a light blue windbreaker. Heels that would have killed a lesser woman. Tight blue skirt. A mouth that smirked in anticipation of mischief and eyes that devoured every detail in the room. Her hair was the only thing different. Instead of blonde she was sporting a long, straight cut of raven's-black, a color that could only have come from a premium dye job.

It was like she had just stepped out of her dorm room, ready to go to class or, more likely, the local pub. This was the friend I remembered.

The look she gave me said she felt the same way about me.

We met in the middle of the floor, hugging each other warmly. I didn't exactly tear up but I'm not afraid to say it was a near thing.

"Let me look at ya!" she said to me, holding me back at arm's length. "Just as beautiful as ever, ain't ya?"

"Look who's talking." I hugged her again. "You haven't changed a bit!"

For just a moment, her eyes were serious. "More than you can know, Dell."

Then she was my old friend Jess again, and I figured I had imagined it.

"This is quite the place, ain't it?" she said, turning around in a circle to take in the whole room. She stopped when she was facing George, looking up at him on top of his ladder. "Hello."

George was still staring, and he knew it, and Jess knew it too. He bobbed his head and raised his hand in greeting.

The painting jumped off the ladder, and fell to the floor with a crash that they probably heard all the way up on the third floor.

I mean it when I say the painting jumped. Anyone else looking at it would have assumed that George caught it with his hand or shoved it with his shoulder accidentally. I knew better. That wall was not going to tolerate anything being put on it. I can't explain it. Ghosts? Maybe. A flaw in the construction? Sure, that would make all the sense in the world.

Except the painting had *jumped* off the ladder.

Not that I could tell that to anyone. Joking with George that nothing is going to stay on that wall is one thing. Telling him straight out that things *fly* and *bounce* away from that wall would get me a one way trip to the nut house.

Besides. Jess just got here. No sense in freaking her out about such things.

Grumbling under his breath in language that made my ears burn, George climbed down the ladder and grabbed the painting, sparing a quick glance for the bent frame before walking out of the room with his head hung low.

Jess laughed softly, placing her hand on my shoulder, and I can't help but laugh with her. Poor George!

"Well, he's a real card, ain't he?" she asks me. "Ah, Dell, I'm so happy that you and Rosie got to live your dream like this. Your own Inn! That's just brilliant. Where is Rosie? She out back in the kitchen? That girl always did love to bake."

I looked through the door to the dining room, knowing Rosie was exactly where Jess figured she was. In the kitchen going over the dinner menu with the wait staff and planning out tomorrow's menu. I also knew that Rosie might not be as excited to see Jess as I was, considering our earlier conversation. Yes. That reunion could wait a bit.

"Tell you what," I said to Jess. "How about we get you set up in your room first and then I'll give you the tour. How's that sound?"

"Sounds perfect. I'm so tired! Sorry it took me so long to get in, Dell. I was on that dirt track they call a road out there and I got distracted by this wonderful little roadside stand selling jellies and little crafts. Oh! That reminds me."

From the pocket of her jacket she took out a leather string, tied like a necklace, with a small wooden charm dangling on the bottom end. Then she handed it to me.

It was a little unicorn, carved in dark teak or some other smooth wood, made to look like it was prancing, his head thrown back and his long and curvy horn pointed at the sky.

"Oh, Jess, that's beautiful."

"It's for you," she tells me. "Just a little thank-you for always being my friend."

"Aw, thanks Jess."

We hug again, and I clutch the necklace in my hand. I always loved unicorns. The myth and the legend, and the way they inspired hope. Other people kept pictures of angels or wore crosses around their neck to remember the promise of hope and love. For me, it was always unicorns.

When I get her the keys for her room from behind the counter I put the cute necklace down next to the cash register. It's just a homemade carving but I love it. I can put it on later. It'll be safe here for now.

We still use real keys here instead of the electronic pass cards that bigger hotels use. When she takes them from me Jess raises an eyebrow, then tucks them both into a pocket of her jacket.

"Do you have any luggage?" I ask her.

The answer is yes, but she wants to get her things later. "For now, just let me pay for the room and then ya can show me where it is."

"You know you don't have to pay me, Jess. We've got empty rooms right now, and you're my friend."

"Ha. If ya let all your friends stay for free you'd be broke in a month, Dell. Here. Run it on this."

She hands me a card from a little wallet she had tucked into her purse. I can't help but notice the name on the card isn't hers. "Steal this, did you?" I asked jokingly.

"No, nothing like that."

She held out her left hand, and it was only then that I saw the rings. Just a small diamond engagement ring and a slim silver band to match, but very pretty.

"Jess! Wow. You and Horace?" Of course. Should've recognized Horace Sapp's name on that card right off.

"Sure enough. Happened a few years ago. He finally popped the question."

As I run his card—her husband's card—I remember how those two were in the last year of Uni. Hot, close, and troubled. Their relationship led to a lot more trouble for Jess, a lot of arguments, and a lot of making up. I gave it six months after graduation.

Looks like I was wrong.

I hand back the card, with another glance at her rings. "So what brings you to Lakeshore? Don't think I had the chance to ask you on the phone."

She shrugged, slipping the card back into her wallet, her eyes distant. "To tell the truth, I wanted to take some time away from Horace. We're married, and that's all well and fine, but marriage don't change some men. He's the same as he's always been. Know what I mean?"

Horace Sapp had been a hard man to understand, sometimes, and truth be told there had been times when he outright scared me. Just now, when I had called their relationship "troubled," I may have been a bit too generous. Volatile would be a better word. I can understand why Jess might need to leave the other side—the mainland—and come down to Tassie for a bit of a rest.

All I could do is smile at her. I've had a husband run out on me, leave me without a trace, but sticking by a man who constantly ran you down and made you cry…well, that probably took more guts than I have. Leaving him might take even more. Jess was at my Inn now. I was going to make sure she didn't have to worry about anyone upsetting her. Nothing bad was going to happen to her. Not while she was here.

"Let's get you settled in," I tell her, coming around from behind the registration desk to hug her again. "We can come back for your bags later. I really want to show off my town to you, too. Got time for a look see tonight?"

"Oh, Dell. I'm feeling a bit stuffed. Could use a rest in a nice soft bed. Show me your Inn first. If I make it up to the room now then I'm just going to bury myself in the blankies and sleep the day away. Plus I want to say hi to Rosie!"

"Well, let's go see her first." I put as much cheerfulness in my voice as I could manage. I think I even kept a straight face when I did. Rosie was already sour on Jess visiting, and now I would get to tell her that our old friend from University was basically running from her husband. That should go over like a lead balloon.

It turned out that Rosie was far too busy baking and mixing to do more than wave to Jess through the swinging half door that separated the kitchen from the dining room. We waved back, and then I took Jess on a quick look around. She was impressed, and told me so several times, which I have to say made my ego swell. Here I'd been worrying what she would think of my little place. I should have known better.

I told her about the three lakes outside of town, and about how beautiful the place is in the warmer months when everything is in bloom. I told her about some of the people here, my friends, and even got to brag about my son Kevin, local police officer. We talked about my Inn some more, about how it's hard sometimes to get in supplies from Geeveston or Hobart in a timely fashion and how we depend on local suppliers for our meats and our jams and our honey. After a while we settled ourselves in the sunroom off the entryway with cups of coffee one of the servers brought to us.

"He was cute," Jess whispered to me after Paul had given us our steaming cups and left the room.

"Jess!" I protested with a smile. "You're a married woman, remember?"

She winked at me, and then hid her expression behind a long sip of her coffee. I know what she means. Paul is our youngest guy server and he looks like that singer, the one all the girls go crazy over with the dark hair and the sparkling eyes. In those tight slacks he wears I've seen more than a few girls watching him walk away. Bit young for me, but that doesn't stop most.

"Sure, I'm married," she sighs, putting the cup down. "That doesn't mean I can't look, right? Besides. Horace isn't here. But we are. We should so hit the town tomorrow, Dell! Be like old times."

"I don't know how old-timey it can be in this town," I told her. "It's not like it is in Sydney. Figured that out right quick when I moved here."

"Ya got a pub, don't ya?"

"Such as it is." I don't go to the Thirsty Roo very much, myself. Still, if Jess was looking for that kind of an outing, it was the best we had to offer. "We could take a trip up to Hobart if you wanted? I can have someone cover the desk for a day."

"Nah, too far to drive. I wore myself out just getting here. Like to stay here in Lakeshore." Suddenly she was yawning, covering her open mouth with the back of one hand. "Speaking of. Time for a bit of a sleep. Think I'll go up to my room."

"I'll help you bring your things up," I offered.

Stretching her arms out she shook her head. "No need. It's locked up in my car out in the lot. I'll get it later."

"Okay. It's room seven. Got your keys?"

She patted her pocket. "Yup. See you later tonight?"

"Sure thing. I've got some errands to run in town that I really should get to. I'll knock on your door for supper. How's that sound?"

"Enph," she muttered through another yawn. "Make it a late supper? Eightish?"

My stomach wanted to growl at the thought of eating so late, and I knew it would mean cold sandwiches unless Rosie had some leftovers in the huge kitchen refrigerator we could warm up. Still, I was just happy to have Jess here. I could hold off eating for a bit if it meant visiting with her some more.

Standing up with her we gave each other another hug. "Glad you're here, Jess."

Death in Room 7

"Likewise, Dell. Wake me for supper. Then we can start to paint this town red."

We both laugh at that joke. Even though I've heard it before. Lots of times.

⁓

Living in Lakeshore means getting used to the color white. A lot of white. Let me explain why.

Australia, including Tasmania, was a dumping ground for criminals' way back in the late 1700s and into the 1800s. They were sent here as slave labor, most of them, and others got sent over just to get them away from the decent folk. 'Course, it wasn't called Tasmania back then. Back then it was Van Diemens Land after the leader of the Dutch East Indies. Wasn't until around 1856 that the name got changed to Tasmania. Guess everyone thought "Van Diemens Land" sounded too much like The Demon's Land.

We already have the Tasmanian Devil as part of our image. I think it's best to stay away from demons and devils altogether.

So anyway. Criminal types got sent here, to Tasmania, and the good Lieutenant Governor David Collins whose portrait George wants to hang so badly in the lobby of my Inn was responsible for making sure they all stayed in line. Thing is, not every criminal wants to stay locked up even when the prison's in such a nice place as this. Whole groups of prisoners escaped to become bandits.

Bushrangers, they were called. Living and thieving and generally causing trouble from out in the bush. In 1813, bushrangers came to Lakeshore. They burned most of the town. Stole the gold from the mayor's house. I've read there were a few deaths.

After they left, the town rebuilt itself. That's the way of it here in Australia. You get knocked down, you get back up. Lakeshore wasn't a rich community back then so the townsfolk used what they had at hand. When the houses and buildings were reconstructed, they painted them with whitewash. White, as far as the eye could see.

Down through the decades Lakeshore has continued to paint its buildings white. Kind of a nod to our history. Lots of history in Australia, and we're proud of it. Still, that's a lot of white all in one town.

My Inn is one of the few exceptions. A sunflower yellow. Pretty, and most people appreciate the change from all of our white. I had to get a special permit just to do it though.

Walking up the street now, past white houses and white stores and our one simple white church, I come to the fountain in the middle of Main Street. I really do have things to take care of but I take a moment to watch the tiny trickle of water coming out at the top of the three tiers. It used to pour out gallons of fresh water, gushing in a tall spray, but in the last few years it's gotten less and less. No one knows why.

I love this town. Ever since I came here I've loved it. Everything about it, even the pathetic cement fountain. It's usually quiet and peaceful here. We have our troubles, but they soon go away. There's nowhere else on Earth I'd rather live than right here. Even when I'm just out running errands.

The Milkbar is my first stop, picking up a few things like shampoo for myself, and some groceries that Rosie needs for a special desert she's making tomorrow. Paper bags in hand I head over to the post office to collect the Inn's mail. Gary the postmaster asks me how business is, and I ask the same of him. "Slow," he says, just like always. "The Internet's gonna kill letters just like video killed the radio star."

That joke is always funny. A little more funny to Gary than it is to me, but still.

Death in Room 7

On my way out of the post office, I see a familiar face coming in.

"Hey, Mom." Kevin smiles at me, tall and strong in his dark blue uniform shirt. His auburn hair used to be down to his shoulders but he's kept it buzzed short since getting hired at Lakeshore's police force.

It was a proud day for me when Kevin came to work here. I let him know about the position as soon as it came open, never thinking he'd actually want to come live in the same town his mom had moved to. He'd always wanted to be a police officer, though, and the timing was right. Now I get to see his freckled face every day. We look a lot alike, me and Kev. Everybody says so.

"Hey there," I say to him, awkwardly balancing my packages and my mail to give him a hug. "Off duty?"

"Yup. My shift ended an hour ago. Just getting the mail and then heading home."

"Stellar! Have time for dinner? A friend of mine from University stopped by. Love for you to meet her."

"Oh, sorry Mom. Can't tonight. I've got a…thing to take care of. Lunch tomorrow?"

"Sounds great." He's hiding something, that's easy enough to see, but boys will be boys and a few secrets never hurt anyone. "I'll see you then."

Another hug, and we go our separate ways. On my way back to the Inn I start whistling. The sun is high in a blue sky streaked by pure white clouds. Birds are calling to each other on a nice, warm breeze. I can't imagine a more perfect day.

Back at the Inn I bring the foodstuffs to the kitchen and put them away. Paul offers to help me but I know his shift is long over and he's only hanging around because he's a dedicated man. Wish I could give him more hours than I do, but the Inn has a budget, so I send him on his way. Have to agree with Jess. He is nice to watch when he's walking away.

Ahem. Guess it's been a while since I had some male companionship of my own. Maybe, I think in passing, it might be time to open myself up to the possibility. Maybe.

Rosie is nowhere to be found. Dinner is in full swing now, and the servers are taking care of everyone just fine, but I can't imagine Rosie leaving her kitchen at a time like this. One of the other servers, a woman about my age in a white shirt and black vest like the rest of them, tells me that Rosie said she had to run home to her husband and left early for the day. I ponder on that as I leave the kitchen. Maybe Josh was sick. Rosie was a very devoted wife. She was devoted to her kitchen too, and usually that took precedence over anything except Armageddon or an outbreak of smallpox. I doubt that Josh has smallpox.

The mail comes with me back to the registration desk. When I'm gone, Rosie is supposed to do double duty as the face of the Inn, here at the desk. I check the sign-in book and see that no one has registered since I've been gone. It really hasn't been all that long, after all. This is about the right number of guests for this time of year. Just enough to make the place cozy and the dining room full of tourists and local residents alike. Summer in Australia is something everyone should experience once in their life.

I get to do it every year of mine.

The unicorn necklace that Jess gave me catches my eye. Smiling, I lengthen the cord just a bit and then slip it on over my neck, putting the unicorn down inside my shirt. I can feel it there, nestling like a little good luck charm.

A few hours pass like they usually do in Lakeshore. Quiet and peaceful. The phone rang twice, with no one there. Just static. I tend to listen to the static more closely nowadays, ever since I started giving serious thought to whether ghosts can use phones to communicate. I never hear anything but white noise, in case you're wondering.

Death in Room 7

At a little past seven-thirty I decide I can't wait for Jess to wake up. I'm hungry. Laughing softly to myself, I head up the stairs hoping she won't be too mad if I wake her up just fifteen minutes earlier than we had agreed on. Of course she won't. What's fifteen minutes between friends?

I knocked on her door. Then I knocked again, a little louder. She didn't answer. Ear to the door I knocked again. "Jess?"

Still no answer. Must still be asleep. She had sounded so tired when she came upstairs. Long drive. Sounded like a lot going on in her life, too. Best to let her rest.

We could always catch up tomorrow.

CHAPTER THREE

My telephone rang in my room early the next morning. Like, early enough that the sun was only a thought on the eastern horizon across the lake.

It kept ringing, and I thought about smashing it to bits with the nearest heavy object. I decided against that plan but only because it would cost too much to replace.

"You're lucky I can't live without you," I mumbled to the annoying little contraption. It's made to look like an antique stand-up style phone even though it has a push-button keypad. There's one in each of the rooms. Just one of the many touches I use to make the place special.

On the next ring I grabbed the receiver up and angrily growled, "Hello. What?"

"Is this Adelle Powers?" a male voice asked me.

"Hmph? Who is this?"

"I said," the man repeated, his tone annoyed, "is this Adelle Powers?"

Something about the phone call made me sit up straight in bed. "I'm Adelle. Most folks call me Dell. Now, who is this?"

"This is Horace Sapp. Don't remember me?"

Now I did. Horace. Jess's boyfriend. Well, husband now. The hazy fog of sleep parted for me and I could recognize the inflection in his voice, the condescending tone he put into every word. Just like back in Uni. I hadn't actually spoken with him since then. Jess and me had spoken a few times, e-mailed and sent cards, too, but I haven't heard from Horace since—

"Are ya still there?"

"Uh, yeah, Horace. I'm still here. It's…" A check of the clock showed me exactly how early it was. Scrubbing my hand over my face I manage to suppress a sigh, and then a yawn. "It's early. What can I do for you?"

"I'm looking for Jess."

Jess had said she was here to take a break from Horace. I just assumed she'd told him where she was going.

Obviously not.

"Uh, shouldn't you just call her mobile, Horace?"

"Tried that. She didn't answer. Funny thing, though. Just got a charge report on me credit card. Seems she just checked into the Pine Lake Inn. So I look online and find out our old friend Adelle Powers runs the place. Surprise, surprise. So. Where's my wife, Adelle?"

Oh, I really do not want to be in the middle of a domestic spat. I should hang up the phone. Hang up, then leave it off the hook, and get back to sleep. That's what I should do. Only, Jess is a friend of mine, and she needs my help. I can't just pretend it's not my problem. Time moves on, but friends are forever. Or at least they should be.

So.

"She was here, Horace. She said something about taking a vacation. I think she mentioned Southport."

There was a long pause on the line, and I very nearly hung up right then. Maybe I should have.

"Adelle, I know she's there. Don't lie to me! So help me, I will come down there and find her meself. Hear me?"

Loud and clear, I think to myself. "Listen, Horace—"

"No! You listen to me. I want to speak to my wife..." Part of what he said was cut off by static. "...she doesn't know..." More static. "...tell her!"

Then a harsh burst of static cut his voice off completely, and there was only white noise. "Hello?" I asked. Nothing. Just static rising and falling, a noise that was oddly soothing. Lulling me back toward sleep.

Horace had sounded pretty furious. That was going to cause some problems for my little Inn if he made good on his threat to come looking for Jess. I sighed, sitting there, listening to a phone call that wasn't there anymore. I had been so happy when Jess came. It was supposed to be so much fun. Now this.

I remembered Rosie saying that Jess brought trouble with her no matter where she went. Maybe this was the proof of that.

Well. Nothing I could do about it tonight. This morning, I mean. Damn, it was early! The static was a soft lullaby in my ear, and I knew that I could at least catch another couple of hours sleep before I had to tell Jess the bad news and get her to give up the whole story of why she was here. There was obviously more to it than she was letting on.

I laid down against the pillow, the phone's receiver still to my ear, and let the hissing, popping, shushing noises lead me toward sleep.

...Night, Dell...

I could almost hear those words whispered in my ear. For some reason, it made me smile.

That's the last thing I remembered until I woke up again, later, with the sun bright in my windows and the alarm clock chirping at me. Seven o'clock. Ah, the glamorous life of a small town Inn keeper. Ha.

Death in Room 7

A shower gets me ready for the day, although a cup of Rosie's coffee will do wonders for my soul. I take out my favorite blue dress to wear, the one with the white down the sides and the black circle at the waist like a wide belt. Then I think better of it and pick out a pair of dark jeans and a loose, breezy black top instead. If I'm going to give Jess a walking tour of the town that winds up with us both at the Thirsty Roo, then I think dressing practical is going to be the order of the day. Best to be prepared for whatever might happen.

Jess. I frown at myself in the bathroom's mirror, and sit on the edge of the tub to tie up my sneakers. She needed to know her husband was on his way, probably, and that he wasn't what you might call in a good mood. Also, I think she owes me a bit of an explanation.

Locking the door behind me, like I tell all my guests to do, I walk downstairs to the second floor and start down the hall to Jess's room.

Mister Brewster is standing in the middle of the hallway.

Maybe it's just coincidence that he's looking right in my direction. He smiles that cold, lifeless smile of his and then turns around, down to his room, and disappears inside.

For a man who doesn't come out of his room much I sure do run into him a lot. Been here a long time, he has. You'd think I'd be used to him by now.

Anyway.

At Jess's door I knock. Then knock again. Oh, come on. "Jess," I call in to her, loudly enough that I probably woke up some of the other guests. I knock a third time, and then once more.

No answer.

With a weary sigh, I have to wonder just what Jess has gotten me into.

I have spare keys to all of the rooms, of course, for emergencies. I know as soon as I turn away and head downstairs that I'm going to get the key from behind the registration desk to let myself in and wake Jess up. No way she was that tired from her drive here.

So why isn't she answering?

Maybe she got up before me and went out on the town. Might be she was even in the dining room eating breakfast. We start serving at six in the morning, just simple fare like scrambled eggs and bacon and pikelets. The regular servers can make all of that up. Rosie comes in early on the weekends and then we have things like dippy eggs and vegemite soldiers.

I look into the dining room, glad to see the small crowd laughing and talking and eating, but Jess isn't there.

Now I really wish I'd gotten her mobile number from her yesterday. I could at least call it and see if she was out and about. Oh. I could call her room. Best to start with that before bursting in on her, I suppose.

Behind the front desk I dial the three digit extension and listen to it ring on the other end. I let it go on for far too long. She's not answering.

A little sense of dread spreads over me. Time to get the key and check her room. The spare keys are on the peg board in the wooden cabinet set into the wall behind me, all in order, on their own hooks, one per room.

The hook for Jessica's room is empty.

As I'm looking over the other keys to make sure it hadn't accidentally got put in the wrong spot I hear the front door open. It's Rosie, all cheerful smiles and whistling some tune I can't identify.

"Morning, Dell," she says to me. "The hubby and I had the grandest time last night. I was thinking of trying that new soup for lunch we talked about. What do ya think?"

She sees the look on my face and tilts her head to one side. "Hey. What's wrong?"

I tell her about the phone call from Horace, and about how I can't get Jess to answer the door to her room, and about the missing key from the pegboard. If ever a woman's face so plainly said "I-told-you-so" it's hers, right now.

"Well," she says out loud. "She's probably out on the town, like you thought. Let's give her a bit and then panic after that."

"I don't know." I lean on the edge of the registration desk, tapping my fingers, thinking. "If Horace is on his way here now it seems we should find Jess sooner, rather than later."

"Or we could just let her problems belong to her," Rosie suggests.

I study my friend's expression, trying to read what I see there. This isn't like Rosie. She's usually nice to everyone, happy to give everyone the benefit of the doubt and go out of her way to help. Now that Jess is here it's like someone spit in her porridge.

She turns under my scrutiny and heads straight for the kitchen. "I'm sure she'll turn up. Ooh. Turnips. In the soup. Perfect!"

"Rosie, come on," I plead with her. "Jess is our friend. What's wrong with you?"

She stops, her back still facing me, tugging at the sleeves of her white blouse. "Maybe Jess and me were never the good friends that you thought we were."

"What? What does that mean?"

After a quiet moment where I can hear the clock ticking and the drone of conversation in the dining room, Rosie turned to look up the stairs. "It means we probably should go check on her." She didn't quite look back at me as she added, "Dell, there's some things you should know 'bout Jess. Things I never said back at University, 'cause you and she were such good friends."

"Rosie? What are you talking about?"

Her gaze went back up to the stairs. "I'm saying…I'll tell ya later. Let's go check on her."

It wasn't said with a lot of enthusiasm, and I still wanted to know what Rosie was talking about that could have been so bad, but that tingly feeling all up and down my back was still there, and I decided we could wait to talk about the old times. I needed to see if Jess was still in her room. If she wasn't, my first instinct was to call Kevin up and have him and some of his police buddies go looking for her around town. She couldn't have gotten far. I had seen her car still in the parking lot through one of the windows.

Besides the spare keys to the rooms, I have a master key as well, something every smart Inn owner should have in case of a guest who doesn't want to leave or such. That's in the wooden cabinet, too, behind the peg board, with the keys to the rental car I keep for the Inn and a few other things as well. Swinging the peg board out I get that key, close the cabinet up, and start upstairs with Rosie.

She doesn't say anything to me the whole time. Her lips are pressed tightly together in a frown. In fact she looks like a woman on her way to her judgment. Maybe I should have asked her before agreeing to let Jess come and stay here. I just never thought it would be this much trouble. She's my friend. That's all that should matter.

I'm not sure Rosie would agree with me.

At Jess's door I insert the key and then wait, knocking one last time, calling out to her again, telling her we're coming in and she'd better be decent.

The joke falls flat when there's still no answer. I look at Rosie. Her eyes are a little unfocused, her expression grim, as if she knows what we're going to find in there. For a moment I hesitate, not sure I want to know what Rosie apparently already suspects.

Gathering my courage against…well, I really didn't know what, I pushed the door open.

The smell hit me first. A coppery tang mixed with damp wetness. There's only one thing in the world smells like that.

Blood.

Then I saw her.

Rosie lifted her hand to her mouth with a gasp and then turned away. I couldn't. Turn away, I mean. I couldn't turn away.

Jess sat in the room's only chair, over in the corner by the window. She sat very stiff, and very pale. She was still wearing the clothes she had on yesterday. Like she'd never even gone to bed.

On the floor at her feet were pools of drying blood. Streaks of it ran down her arms from the uneven, jagged cuts in both wrists. Her eyes were open, staring at the ceiling, her head rolled back.

Jess was dead.

Nausea broke over me in waves as I slowly closed the door again. I made sure to lock it with my master key and then I took Rosie by the hand. Together we went downstairs silently, without a word, to call my son.

It was time to call the police in.

⁓

"Didya check for a pulse?" Senior Sergeant Cutter asked me in the second floor hallway. For the fifth time.

Angus Cutter was a tall and muscular man. I've always suspected he had been a body builder, once upon a time. His white hair was shaved close down to his scalp. His face was clean shaven except for that white handlebar mustache he sported that framed up his square jaw. Gold clusters sat on the shoulder lapels of his stiff blue uniform shirt.

The man looked like a bull who'd learned to walk upright. He had the personality to match. Blunt, direct, and narrow minded.

"Senior Sergeant, I told you. I opened her door with my master key. When I saw…what I saw, I closed the door again and called you."

Also for the fifth time, he scratched that information down in his little spiral notebook. Then he shook his head and put notebook and pen away in the front pocket of his shirt. "Right. Then. Looks to be cut and dry to me, Dell. Sorry 'bout your friend. Sometimes people end it. Just the way of the world."

Rosie came up the stairs just as I was wondering how much time I'd get in a cell for slapping a cop across his stupid face. She took me by the arm and pulled me away from the Senior Sergeant. "I took care of informing all the guests that there was a problem," she said. "I let them know the police would be here for a bit and then gone. No worries."

"Thank you." A problem. That's what we were calling Jess's death. A problem.

In a way, that's exactly what it was. I was so angry at Jess right now that if she was right here with me I would've taken her by the shoulders and shook sense into her until her teeth rattled. She had come here, to my Inn, just to kill herself. Now we had the police coming in and out, and we'd have to wait for two hours before a coroner could come down from Hobart to take the body. There would be an autopsy, of course, because of the way she…died. I'd learned that from Kevin. Sometimes having a police officer for a son came in handy.

Sometimes, I just feel like I know too much.

Anyway, angry as I was at Jess, I was also deeply sad for her. Obviously her marriage with Horace wasn't working. If that phone call I got from him at…what, four thirty this morning? If that phone call was any indication then it's no wonder she had to come here to catch a break. Now this…

A sudden sob choked me. Rosie put her arms around my shoulders and it helped but not enough. Poor Jess. Why? It was so senseless. Why would she do this?

Death in Room 7

As I stood there, another officer came out of the room where Jess's body still sat in that chair. I only knew he was an officer because I recognized his face. He was in jeans and a long-sleeved work shirt, not a uniform. His name escaped me. There was a total of six officers in town, including Senior Sergeant Cutter over there. In a town like Lakeshore everyone knew everyone else.

"Got everything, Senior Sergeant," the officer said to Cutter. Blake Williams. That was his name. He held up a clear plastic bag and in it I could see a bloody razor blade.

My stomach turned over on itself.

"Took the pictures, too," Blake said. "Every inch of the room."

Cutter took the bag with a scowl. "Why'd ya go and waste the time on taking pics? It's clear as the desert sky what happened in there."

Rosie caught me glaring at him. Good to have friends who know when to give you a bit of a hard yank to keep you out of trouble.

Feet came pounding up the stairs. Kevin never did have a very light step. He came right over to me, hugging me fiercely. Me and my son are still very close. In moments like this, I'm glad of it.

"Sorry, Mom. I had my mobile off. I just got your message and came right over and…is she really dead?"

I nodded and started to say something only to have Cutter interrupt.

"You'd know that," he snapped at Kevin, "if ya ever answered that phone of yers. Mind tellin' me why ya weren't where I could get hold of ya when I needed to?"

Kevin met his Senior Sergeant's stare but I could feel the way he tensed up. Things haven't been so good between Cutter and him. Lot of jealousy there, on the Senior Sergeant's part, knowing my Kevin's the better officer. That's not just a mother's pride talking there, either.

"Sorry, Senior Sergeant," Kevin said to him. "Won't happen again."

Smart boy. Don't pick a fight with your boss. Even when you're right.

Cutter rolled his eyes. "Well, yer here now. Might as well make use of ya. I know Dell here's yer rellie and all but I want ya to write out her statement. Think ya can handle it?"

With a thin smile, Kevin answered, "Sure thing."

"Beauty. Go do that downstairs. We'll finish up here."

It was a dismissal, a way for Cutter to get my son away from the scene. He'd been doing that a lot recently, from what I understand, and Kevin was just about fed up with it. He'd put his application in to the Australian Federal Police, and he was just waiting to hear back from them. I'd hate to see him transfer to the national police force, but he was always too good for a small time department like we have here in Lakeshore.

"Kevin," I asked him on the way downstairs, where I could be sure none of the guests would hear us, "why does Cutter need you to take my statement? It doesn't sound like he's interested in doing an investigation."

Just a suicide after all, I added bitterly to myself.

"We still have to follow the book," was his answer. "Don't worry. I'll make sure there's an investigation. The autopsy might tell us something more than what we already know. Let me ask you some questions, too."

"Like what?" Rosie asked from behind us.

"Like, was the door locked when you got to her room?"

"Yes," I answered him. "We had to use our master key to get in."

"Dell, tell him," Rosie urged. We were at the bottom of the stairs now and we made sure to keep our voices down so that none of the guests who might be in the dining room or the commons would hear us. "Tell him about the keys."

"Oh, right. I'd nearly forgotten."

Kevin waited, watching us both, then scratched at the back of his neck. "Er, mom, I've never been psychic."

I chuckled in spite of myself. Kevin could always make me feel better. "Rosie means the keys to the rooms. The key to Jess's room, more to the point. You see—"

"Where is me wife!" a loud, familiar voice boomed out from the front door.

A deep breath did nothing to calm me down. Horace was here. Perfect.

Kevin stepped up and put himself in the path of Jess's irate husband. He was as tall as I remembered. Taller than my Kevin, to be sure. In University he had always been an athlete, strong and lean, every girl's dream of a perfect man. A real spunk. The muscles were still there, but over the years he'd packed on more than a few pounds to his midsection. The beer belly strained the material of his white cotton shirt.

His looks were slipping, too. What had once been a full head of wavy black hair was now a comb over trying to hide a huge bald spot. Permanent scowl lines had been etched in around his eyes and mouth.

Rosie stepped in behind the registration desk. Couldn't blame her, considering the dangerous look in Horace's murky hazel eyes. I wondered if she felt the same way about Horace as she did about Jess. If she didn't, I had enough distrust of the man for both of us.

He stopped halfway across the room when Kevin made it obvious he wasn't going to move out of the way. "Can I help you?" he asked in that professional police officer voice he has.

"Help me? Doubt it, bucko. Unless you're hiding me wife in your back pocket. That it? She come here to see you?"

Kevin didn't rise to the bait. "You must be Jess's husband?"

"Well don't you catch on quick? Step aside. Jess!"

"No need to shout," Kevin said calmly. "My name's Constable Kevin Powers. Let's go in the next room. We need to talk."

"I don't want to have a convo, you bloody walloper!" Horace reached out and shoved Kevin by the shoulder. "I'm here for me wife!"

With practiced, smooth movements, Kevin put himself behind Horace, taking a firm grip on that one arm, twisting it up and back and using it like a lever to walk the man up against the wall.

"Hey! Leggo!"

Kevin held Horace in place without any effort at all. He never raised his voice, never threatened. He was simply calm and professional. He might have been holding a stray cat in his arms for all the world to see. "We need to talk first. There's been an incident."

"An...?" All the wind blew out of Horace's sails all at once. "Tell me where Jess is. You tell me where she is! Did something happen to her?"

"I'll tell you everything I know," Kevin promised. "In the next room. I'm going to let go of your arm now, and you and me will have a sit down. All right?"

Horace nodded, his eyebrows narrowing, finally catching on that there was something going on here at the Inn, and that he wasn't in control. "Uh, sure, Officer. Just tell me what's going on. I'm here for Jess."

As promised, Kevin let go, and motioned for Horace to go ahead of him into the commons room. They sat down on the couch in there, out of my view.

"How'd he get here so fast?" Rosie wondered out loud, still behind the desk, talking quietly enough that only I could hear her.

That was a good question. Unless he'd already been heading this way when I got that call, he shouldn't have arrived until late afternoon at the earliest. He must have been on his way. On the road. A lot closer than I had thought.

Only to find Jess dead when he got here.

The irony of that didn't escape me. I just didn't want to dwell on it.

"So what now?" Rosie asked me.

"For now, it's business as usual," I suggested. "We still have guests to take care of. What happened to Jess…I hate it. I hate everything about it. Doesn't mean we get to close up shop. As much as I'd like to pack it in for a few days until everything's over, we can't. We both have bills to pay."

She nodded, her expression full of understanding. "Why don't ya take the rest of the day off, at least? I can run things for that long."

I knew she could, but the last time I let her take over for a day we had to replace two tables in the dining area that somehow caught fire. Besides, working would give me something to do to take my mind off seeing Jess in that chair, with the blood on the floor, and that look on her face…

I could still picture it in my mind, in perfect detail.

Every detail.

Wait.

Now that I was calmer, I realized something. Something about the blood. I couldn't be right. In my mind I knew I had to be wrong.

But I wasn't.

"Uh, Rosie, I need to run back upstairs for a minute. Thanks for the offer to watch things today but I'd rather be here. Oh," I said, remembering something else. "What was it you were going to tell me about Jess? Remember, from earlier? You said there was something I didn't know about her?"

"Oh, my. This isn't the time, Dell. Ask me again later. Don't see how it could matter now, anyways."

Maybe it didn't, but if I was right about what I had seen in the room, where Jess died, then it might mean more than either of us realized.

From the commons room, a terrible shout broke the silence. There were no words in it, just the sound of anguish. Kevin must have told Horace about Jess.

CHAPTER FOUR

Kevin kept Horace downstairs. Probably by telling him that the room his wife was in was a crime scene now and he'd be able to see his wife after the Coroner had removed her. I wasn't sure how long that would keep Horace away, but hopefully it would be long enough.

I went back up the stairs two at a time, knowing I had to look back in that room quickly before Cutter and Blake did something to change things. I had to see it, again, for myself.

At the door to the room I knocked, then stepped right in like I owned the place. Which I do, if we want to get technical.

"Are you nuts?" the Senior Sergeant demanded, his voice raising with each word. "This is a crime scene! Get out!"

"Oh, right, sorry," I said, playing the sweet, innocent woman. "Didn't mean to muck anything up. Just wanted to let you know that her husband is downstairs."

"Great, just what I need." Cutter threw his hands in the air and paced back and forth.

In that moment I saw what I needed to see. I looked over at Jess. She was so pale and stiff. Tears stung my eyes but I forced myself to look down at the blood on the floor.

There was a puddle of it around her feet. That was to be expected when someone bled out, I'm sure. That could be explained by a suicide.

The spatters of blood that trailed away from her chair, across the pale brown rug on the floor, and then up the wall to the windowsill definitely could not be explained by a woman who sat in a chair to slowly cut away at her wrists.

I ran the scene through my mind in several ways, hating myself for being so cold and logical when my friend was sitting in a chair, right there, dead. No matter how I tried to picture it there was no way I could explain the bloodtrail to the window. Not if Jess had killed herself by cutting her wrists.

It didn't add up.

Which meant only one thing.

"Come on, Dell," Cutter said, walking up to me and pushing me—not very gently—back into the hall. "Blake, stay out here and make sure no one else goes in that room until the Coroner shows up. Hear me?"

"Yes, Senior Sergeant." Blake followed us out, too, and then shut the door so I couldn't see inside anymore. Didn't matter. I found what I was looking for. Not what I had wanted to see, but what I needed to see.

Jess hadn't killed herself.

Someone had done it for her.

I held my trembling fingers over my mouth and let Cutter direct me to the stairs and down. This day was quickly becoming a nightmare. Cutter had to know about this, didn't he? Not even a yobbo like him could have missed that.

"Senior Sergeant Cutter, did you see...?"

"I want you to let the Coroner into that room when he gets here." He spoke right over me, ignoring my question entirely. "Understand? We'll get your Inn back to ya in short order. No worries."

"That's not what I'm worried about," I tried explaining.

"Right. So. I'll go have a convo with whomajigger now. Jess's husband. What was his name?"

"Horace, but—"

"Right. Be a good sheila and bring us some tea, right?"

Oh, he did not just call me a sheila. I am so going to slap that stupid look right out of his eyes!

"Mom," Kevin called to me from the front door, motioning me over to him. I guess he could see the intention written on my face, and once again he saved his mother from doing something she might have to explain in front of a judge.

"Kevin," I hissed, not even at a whisper.

"I know Cutter's hard to take, Mom, but you can't just—"

"Nevermind him! I need to tell you something. I don't think Jess killed herself!"

"I know."

That answer made me feel faint. "What do you mean, you know?"

He pulled me out onto the front porch and pulled the door closed behind us. "I was just talking to Horace. Not a nice bloke."

"I kind of figured that out. I knew him before, you know. Hasn't changed a bit. He called here this morning, before dawn, demanding to know where Jess was."

"That so?" He nodded several times, and I could see him sorting information in his mind. "Interesting."

"Interesting? How's that?"

"Because," he said. "I think someone did kill Jess. And I think Horace was that someone."

At the same time, we both looked in through the window, to where Senior Sergeant Cutter was talking with Horace. His eyes turned toward us, as if he could feel us watching him, and there was something in them I can't quite describe. Something dark.

Something murderous.

When my son came home from school one day and told me that he wanted to be a police officer, it was one of the happiest days of my life. I was so proud of him. Worried, too, because what mother wouldn't be, but that didn't keep me from framing a picture of him in his police uniform his first day on the job here in Lakeshore.

Even so, there's been times when I wish he'd picked a different career. Cutting stones in the quarry outside of town. Becoming a fisherman in Sydney. Moving to the States and going to work in Hollywood, even. He had the face for it.

As a police officer, he sees a lot of the bad things in life. People doing bad things. Robbing. Lying.

Murder.

'Course, this time I got to see the evil that men do to each other firsthand. My own friend, killed in a room at my Inn. It was just too much.

The coffee was helping. It was the middle of the afternoon and in Lakeshore that meant that most people were either at home or at work. I should be at work. I just couldn't bring myself to be in the building right now. I know I told Rosie that I wouldn't take the rest of the day off but after finding out that Jess's death was actually her murder, I had to get some air.

That, and pick my son's brain for what the police were going to do about it.

At least we were alone in Cindy Morris's Milkbar, just me and him and Cindy over behind the deli counter slicing up meat to make some of her famous sandwiches. She always had a few wrapped and ready for people stopping through for something quick to eat.

Tall coolers stood along the walls around us, filled with cold drinks and cold cuts and other assorted perishables. Rows of shelves on the one side displayed canned food products and dry goods like flour and salt. Me and Kevin sat at one of the three round tables Cindy had in place for folks who wanted to sit and have a meal here. She did a pretty brisk business in this little store of hers. It was the town's grocery store and deli and gossip bar all in one. She'd had the walls painted white to match the outside not too long ago, and the wood floors had been waxed just last month. Cindy took good care of her place.

"You and I both know Cutter's gonna try and sweep this under the rug," Kevin said after swallowing a bite of his vegemite sandwich. "He'd rather take the easy answer than dig in the dirt."

"We all know that. How that man keeps his job is beyond me."

"He must be very well connected, have friends in high places." He shrugged it off. "That's the way of it sometimes. Corruption happens everywhere."

I was a little surprised at his casual acceptance of the situation. "Someday that'll change." I really, really hope I'm right in that.

"Maybe," Kevin admits, "but that day isn't today. Right now I need to find proof that Horace killed your friend."

"What did he say to you?"

Putting his sandwich down, Kevin brushed crumbs off his hands, giving me that look I know so well. "You know I shouldn't be telling you 'bout this."

"Yes, but you're going to tell me anyway."

"Because you're just going to keep pressing me until you find out."

That, at least, makes me smile. "You know me so well."

"The great Dell Powers. To know her is to love her." He took a sip of his soft drink before leaning his elbows on the table, closer to me, so I could hear him as he lowered his voice. "Horace is one right tosser, I can tell ya that. Tosser with a capital T. He's upset, and he's angry, but I don't get a sense that he's sad that Jess is dead."

"I tell you, Kevin, from what he said to me over the phone I wouldn't have been surprised to see the two of them come to blows."

"Maybe they did."

I could only nod my head in agreement. "I was thinking the same thing. Maybe he got to the Inn this morning, early. Maybe even right after he called. For all I know he might have called from my parking lot."

"That's what I was thinking. Except, go another step further. Maybe he got here before his phone call. Then he gets into Jess's room, they have a bit of a blue. They have go at each other, and he kills her. Makes his call to you, hey I'm on my way in, where's my wife, blah blah blah, and poof. Instant alibi."

That idea hadn't occurred to me. Could someone be so devious, so…evil, that they could commit a murder, then try to cover it up by pretending to be somewhere else?

Of course they could.

My hand found the string of the unicorn necklace, and pulled the little charm out of my shirt. I held it tight as I thought about it.

"Wouldn't I have seen him? Coming into the Inn?"

"Where were you last night?" he asked, all police business.

I thought back. It seemed like a lifetime ago. "In bed. I went to bed early."

He nodded to that. "And Rosie?"

"She left early. Came in late." Oh, snap. Anyone coulda snuck into the Inn. Including Horace.

Kevin was watching me, waiting for me to make the same connections that he obviously had already made. "But if they had a fight," I wondered, "wouldn't there be bruises on her?"

He shook his head. "Maybe yes, maybe no. Bruises take time to show up. Plus, they don't show up after death. A person's blood needs to be flowing for their skin to bruise. Jess's was…"

"Spilling out onto the floor," I finish for him.

"Right. Sorry."

"No, it's all right. I have to deal with this. It kind of happened in my own house. So. Horace could've beaten her up and then killed her."

"That's the theory." He drummed his fingers on the table. "Except."

"Except? Except what?"

"Well, there's a couple of things that don't add up."

"Like?"

"For one," he said, "how did Horace get into her room? Did she just let him in and then quietly let him beat her up?"

"That's actually two things," I point out, "not one. How did he get in the room, and how could they have a fight without anyone hearing it."

The corner of his mouth curled. "You shoulda been the cop. That's some brilliant deduction. You always did like solving puzzles. So, yes. Take the first part of it, then. How'd he get into the room?"

"Oh! That's what I was going to tell you earlier. The spare key to Jess's room is missing."

Kevin's eyes widened. "Really? Well, that's a stroke of luck then, isn't it?"

"Luck? Why?"

"Find that key…"

"Find the killer," I said, catching on. "We could search Horace's luggage and his car and his blooming pants pockets!"

"Not without a search warrant."

"You don't need a warrant," I pointed out, "if he gives you permission."

"He's not going to give us permission."

He sounded so certain. "Why not?"

"Because if Horace is a killer," he said, slowly, "then he ain't gonna just let me feel around in his pockets for the key to the victim's room."

"Oh. Right." I felt foolish. Foolish, and older than I'd ever felt in my forty-plus years. Not old. Just older. "So our killer has the key, more than likely, we just can't go looking for it without a judge giving us permission. Fine. We'll get a judge's permission."

"We'll try," he shrugged.

Frustration started to slip over me. "So what was the other thing that was bothering you?"

Tearing off a corner of his sandwich he popped it into his mouth and chewed around his words. "See, it kinda goes in hand with the other problem. How did they have a fight without anyone hearing them? That's the question, but more to the point," and here he leaned in closer still, "how did Horace make her sit still so he could cut her wrists?"

I blinked at that image. I hadn't even thought of that. Why would Jess sit still to be killed? There hadn't been one cut, there had been dozens. For that matter, after her wrists were cut why would she sit in one place and just…die?

With a little shake of my whole self I pushed my lunch aside. I sure wasn't hungry anymore. "So, lots of questions to be answered. There must be something else that made you suspect Horace? Something other than how not upset he was by her death?"

"There was. Just not sure I should say."

"That's fine," I told him with a pleasant smile. "I already know about it, anyway."

"What?" he asked, obviously surprised. "Did Jess tell ya 'bout their money troubles?"

He's so cute when I surprise him. Makes his accent come out stronger. "Ah. So, Horace had a motive."

Closing his eyes, he let out a slow breath. "You didn't know about that, did ya? Not until I just said it?"

I shrugged one shoulder. "I still know how to get my son to tell me things, thank you very much."

"Sneaky woman."

"Your mother." I'll take that compliment any day.

"Fine. Horace made sure to tell me, more'n once, that he and Jess were in serious debt. He blames her for it. Says she ran up crazy debts and never told him where the money went. Said she stole his credit card two days ago. That's how he tracked her here."

"She did have Horace's card." I hated to admit that to Kevin. It was like I was ratting on Jess, even though she was dead. "She checked in with it."

"I'll need a copy of that receipt," he told me, pouncing on what was probably a good piece of physical evidence. "I just hope Cutter bagged up anything Jess had in that room. Horace's card included. That'll show he had a motive. The missing key and the fuzzy time frame would give him opportunity."

"Now we just need to figure out the means." Another thing I've learned from having a copper for a son. Means, motive, opportunity.

How did he get Jess to sit still like that, and let herself be killed?

"Find that out, add all of that up with the way he reacted when I told him Jess was dead, and I think we've got our man."

"Our murderer," I corrected.

"Don't worry, mom," he promised, true concern in his voice. "We'll get this bloke. He won't get away with it."

The Milkbar door opened and closed, and when I looked up to see who it was I couldn't keep from groaning. Kevin saw him, too, and quickly stood up from his seat, downing the rest of his drink as he did. "I'd better go. Talk to you soon as I know more, right?"

He wasn't fast enough. The man was already at our table. "G'day, Kevin. Not leaving already, are ya?"

James Callahan was a reporter for the Lakeshore Times. Serving Lakeshore, Geeveston, and the surrounding areas, the paper had run in this town for decades. James had only been at it for the last fifteen years or so. He was my about my age tall and slim and always quick with a smile. Truth was, I didn't hate the man. Actually kind of enjoyed talking to him, on occasion. Just not when I'm trying to discuss the murder of a good friend with my son.

Now there's a sentence you hope never to say twice in your life.

"Hiya, Dell," he said to me, and for just a moment his liquid blue eyes were looking at me to the exclusion of the rest of the world. He was the kind of guy friend a woman always felt close to, even though she knew he was just a friend.

Not me. I mean other women. I suppose. Ahem.

Didn't mean he wasn't cute, with that sandy blonde hair and those dimples that came out when he smiled. He was usually dressed in casual clothes, khakis and button-up shirts, but today he looked like he'd dressed in a careless hurry. His shirt was untucked, his pants wrinkled, and I was almost certain I'd seen two different colored socks on his feet.

"So, Constable Powers," he said to Kevin. "Can I get the scoop on what's happening over at the Pine Lake Inn?"

"You know I have to refer you to Senior Sergeant Cutter," Kevin answered him in a clipped tone. "Most I can tell ya is that my mother runs a fine establishment where many folks have enjoyed a room and a meal and a nice time."

"Can I quote that?" James asked.

"Sure. Knock yourself out." Kevin rolled his eyes over to me, and waved as he walked out of the Milkbar.

I gave half a thought to leaving myself, but James came and sat down across from me, in the seat that Kevin had just vacated, and took a small recorder out of his pocket. "Don't suppose you'd care to make a comment?"

"Sure," I offer. When he held the recorder eagerly out to me, I smiled and said, "I really do have a fine establishment."

He pursed his lips and turned the recorder off. "Now, we both know that's true. Rosie's pikelet's are the best around. Not the news I was aiming for."

"You heard about the death at the Inn?"

"Whole town's heard about it. Thought maybe you'd have something more to say. Seeing as, well, you know. Was it really your friend that died?"

Sharp sadness filled me again. "Yes, James, it was. You can understand why I don't want to talk about it?"

"Sure can." Lifting the little gray recorder up for me to see, he slowly put it away into the side pocket of his khakis. "Tell me 'bout yer friend. What was she like?"

"I'm not going to give you her life to print in the paper," I tell him, a little more harshly than I'd meant to.

If he was offended by my tone, he hid it well. "I'm not asking 'bout her as a reporter. Just looked like ya need to talk. That's all. So tell me. What was she like, this friend of yours?"

For a moment I couldn't speak at all. For him to set everything aside like that and give me the opportunity to express my grief, well, it was like a gift. I hadn't expected that.

"I don't know where to start."

He nodded his head with a bit of a smile, like he understood completely. "Just start from the beginning."

So I did. Meeting Jess at University, at a party at some weirdo's dorm room. From there, everything had just sort of fallen into place for us. The words kept coming, and James sat there with me, nodding his head, or laughing at the funny bits.

I discovered this was exactly what I needed. I needed to tell someone how much Jess meant to me. I needed someone to know her for the vibrant, amazing woman she had been in life. I needed that more than the world just now. James gave me the chance to unburden my soul without ever interrupting me once.

A hard lump of pain that had settled inside my heart worked its way loose and fell away. I took a deep, deep breath when it did.

We stayed there in the Milkbar for the better part of a half hour, and when I'd said everything I could possibly say about Jessica Sapp, James reached over to pat my hand gently. "I feel like I know her myself after all that," he said to me.

I know what he means. It was almost like I was with my good friend Jessica Sapp, just one more time.

"Jess was easy to get to know," I said. "Time was when she had quite the rep for trouble. Got into more'n a few things she shouldn't have. Nothing big, mind you. Just the sort of things that got her lumped in with the bad kids."

"Were you a bad girl?"

For some reason, his question made my cheeks heat up. I'm too old to blush. Aren't I? "No, I wasn't any kind of a bad girl. Jess was always way out in front of what the rest of our group would do. She was my friend, and she was a good one. Didn't matter to me what people said about her."

I scrunch my brow in thought. Rosie sure seemed to be worried about what kind of girl Jess had been. Or, still was. I wondered if maybe my business partner had heard something I hadn't, some rumor that put Jess in a bad light, all those years ago.

She'd promised to tell me, before we got all sidetracked. I suddenly had the feeling that I really needed to hear what Rosie had to say.

"James, thank you for sitting with me," I tell him. I went to stand up, and that was when I noticed his hand was still on mine. It felt kind of nice. When I looked up into his eyes, they were a darker blue then I remembered. More stormy, like there were thoughts going on behind them that were heating his blood.

Ahem. Right. That might be something I needed to look into some other time. I mean, not literally look into, like I was doing right now, in those intense blue spheres, but…wow. Got myself turned around there for a moment.

I can't say that I didn't enjoy it.

But I do take my hand back from his, and stand up from the table. He stands up with me and for a moment I'm tongue tied.

"If you hear anything," he says, "about what happened to Jess, I mean, will you call me?"

"As a reporter?"

He shook his head, eyes still on me. "Not if you're looking for a friend."

"I have to go," I say to him, dodging the entire conversation and knowing that's exactly what I'm doing, but unable to help it. James and I have been something close to friends for years, but I've never thought of taking it further with him. Maybe it was the sting of what my ex-husband had done to me, or maybe it was just fear of taking that leap again. I don't know.

Leaving him there at the table, I told myself it didn't matter. Right now, I had to figure out why Jess had been killed.

And how.

CHAPTER FIVE

I need to talk to Rosie.

Whatever she had been trying to tell me had been something she'd kept a secret since University, apparently, a secret that had bothered her so much that she hadn't even wanted Jess to come to the Inn.

Before, that had just seemed like an old kerfuffle. Now that Jess was dead it seemed like it might be something more. Something important.

It was after four o'clock now. The dinner rush would be about to start at the Pine Lake Inn. A lot of the locals enjoyed having dinner with us. Rosie put on quite a spread, for the guests staying with us, and whoever else wanted to drop in. If I went to talk to her now she'd be too busy to pull herself away from the kitchen, and I didn't want to be responsible for another disaster like we had with the trout sauce a few weeks back. Her focus should be on cooking, not on whatever secret she'd been afraid to tell me all these years.

So. Talking to Rosie would have to wait. If the coroner hadn't made it here yet, he would soon, but the officer stationed on the second floor of the Inn would take care of that. I'd just as soon not see Jess carted out in a black body bag, anyway.

With no reason to go back to the Inn I decided to catch back up with Kevin and see if he'd found anything out in the time I'd spent talking with James. Maybe he'd been able to get a judge's warrant to search Horace's person and belongings. I agreed with him that the key to Jess's room was…well, the key. We needed to find it.

The police department was a long walk from the center of town. Lakeshore might be a small place but it was still twenty minutes or so from end to end by foot. At the westernmost edge of Lakeshore, at the far end of Main Street where pavement gave way to Kookaburra Road again, the houses gradually became fewer as the Monterey Pines grew taller and thicker together. There were a few storage buildings out this way, and Oliver Harris's towing and recovery business, and the police station.

The one story building was made of white stucco and red brick. The bricks had been painted white too, once upon a time, in keeping with the rest of the town, but the whitewash kept coming off in the rains so the town had stopped paying for it to be redone. The white still clung in odd places and made faint outlines of faces and shapes when you weren't looking too closely.

A round sign on the front of the station displayed the town emblem, the silhouette of a pine tree in the middle of our three differently shaped blue lakes. Pine Lake, Gallipoli Lake, and Lake Bowen. It wasn't a big building but then again it had never needed to be very big. Lakeshore was a small town, with small town problems, and a small police force to go with it. If we needed more police presence we called in the Australian Federal Police.

I really hope it doesn't come to that.

The front door was a thick wooden thing. Its hinges squealed a long note of protest as I went in. The lobby was small too, just like the building, with three plastic orange chairs against the wall facing the service window and its sliding glass. The counter had a little metal bell to ring because the front desk was never manned. The police force didn't have the luxury of hiring a secretary.

I rang the bell twice, and then stood there reading the posters on the walls about missing children and the evils of drugs. I didn't have long to wait. I just wish it had been someone else who answered the bell.

Senior Sergeant Angus Cutter stared at me. No. Glared at me. His blue uniform shirt was pressed and pleated and his badge shone like he'd just polished it. Pompous man with a head as hard as Ayer's Rock, but he's our Senior Sergeant. He blew out a breath through his white handlebar mustache before he opened the sliding window for me.

"Can't say I care much for your timing, Miss Powers, but glad you're here. Come on in."

"You're glad I'm here?" Well, that was new. And I was Miss Powers now? What happened to calling me Dell? "Why?"

He quirked one eyebrow at me, and his smile got smarmy. "Because I'm just now arresting your son for murder."

Cold crawlies wormed their way up my spine. A ringing in my ears drowned out Cutter's next words. Murder? My son?

Jess.

Oh…snap.

"You're arresting Kevin for killing Jess?" The words burned in my mouth. My son? "He's a police officer, for the love of God! Like you!"

"Don't matter. Knew yer son was a no gooder. Always knew it. Now I caught him trying to muck up evidence and he won't tell me where he was last night. Two and two still makes four, even for us Taswegians."

"Cutter, you nit! You didn't even think this was a murder! You called it a suicide and practically rushed me out of my own Inn!"

He shrugged both shoulders in a way that told me he couldn't care less what I thought. "That was then. This is now. Your son showed me it was murder, then tried to put the blame on the vic's hubby. Tried to foul up the evidence, too. Know what? Maybe it is good yer here. Maybe you can talk some sense into him. Get him to confess. Be best for him, after all."

The cold gripping at my heart began to melt away under the heat of a fierce anger. My hands fisted up at my sides. "Cutter, I swear I'll see you bounced out of that uniform. I swear it on every Bible in every dresser drawer in my Inn. I'll get you bounced out of this office. Out of this town! I'll get you bounced so far you won't be within cooee of the Northern Territory!"

Cutter waited for me to finish. Then, very calmly, he leaned forward on the windowsill. "Just try it. Have a go. Pretty sure it will take more than one crazy lady to get me removed but have at it. Do your worst."

Then he winked and slammed the glass window closed. I watched him walk away, wishing I could think of something to say to wipe that smirk off his face. A second later he had the door that led from the entry to the offices open for me. I stormed past him with my blood boiling. My only concern now was my son. I can think up nasty things to say to Senior Sergeant Cutter later.

After all, you should never get into a battle of wits with a moron. Both of you lose.

I've been inside the station before. Hard not to, seeing as how my son is one of the handful of officers. Maybe in the big cities like Sydney they have tighter security for their police stations. Here, everyone knows everyone else, and what's marked as confidential in a file is the same thing floating around the rumor mill around town. Not much need for security checks and metal detectors here.

The open inner office has its filing cabinets and wooden console desk with radio equipment and telephones. Also has this old green couch with duct tape covering the rips in it. I doubt this room has changed much since the previous Senior Sergeant was here years ago.

I was expecting him to have me wait on that couch, but instead he brought me down the hall to the door to his office. The surprise must've shown on my face.

"Your son's in here, Miss Powers. I'm just gonna let the two of ya have a nice chit-chat. Tell him it will go easier on him if he just confesses, right?"

"Is there some reason you won't call me Dell?" I snap at him.

"Too right, there is." He opens the door for me with an overdone wave of his hand. "It'd mean we were friends. You two talk. I'll be back in a bit."

He glared at Kevin, inside, before closing the door. There was a lot of hate in that man's eyes.

Kevin sat on this side of the desk. He was sort of sagging in the chair with his hands held loosely in his lap. When he saw me, he shakes his head. He doesn't say anything, though. Not until the door is closed. Not that it should matter. Cutter's probably listening on the other side of the door anyway. Truth be told I wouldn't put it past him to have the office bugged.

When the door closes, Kevin's words nearly break my heart.

"Mom, I didn't do this."

"You think you've got to tell me that?"

He shrugged, head still hung low. "Just thought ya should hear it straight from the source."

Standing up, he hugs me, and I hug him back. "Never doubt your mother," I remind him. At least I got a laugh out of him.

"I'll remember that."

"Now. What's this Cutter's going on about?" I ask him, sitting on the edge of the Senior Sergeant's desk, hoping my backside is making a mess of the neat piles of paperwork there.

Kevin rubs a hand up over his bristle-short hair. "He's gone daft, Mom. He brought me in here an hour ago, and I thought it was from the report I wrote for him. The blood trail from the victim… sorry, from Jess to the window, the things Horace said. Put it all down on paper for him, suggested we needed a warrant to look for the missing key, all that. So he brings me in, sits me down, and outta the blue he starts asking me where I was last night."

"So you told him what?"

"I didn't tell him, actually. None of his business. But then he got this look on his face like he just got me over at chess or something. Starts telling me he knows I messed with the evidence and I need to confess or he'll bury me. He's lost it."

"Yes, and we both know why, don't we?"

We didn't have to say it. Ever since the arrests of Roy Fittimer and Alec Beaudoin last year, where Kevin got more of the credit than Cutter, he'd been on the Senior Sergeant's hit list. Those were both high profile media events for Lakeshore. A drug dealer working most of southern Australia, and a murderer. Kevin had come away looking like the hero no matter how he tried to pass the glory to the Senior Sergeant. It was Kevin who got interviewed on SBS. It was Kevin's quotes in the papers. Senior Sergeant Cutter had been just a footnote.

He'd had been looking for a reason to get rid of Kevin ever since. Looks like he found one.

"He thinks I made up the stuff in Horace's statement," Kevin told me. "As if. Won't listen to reason, either."

"Why won't you just tell him where you were last night? That would end the whole thing right quick. Put him in his place. Give him nothing to hold over you."

My son's face doesn't usually turn that particular shade of scarlet. It did now. "See, it's not just my secret to keep."

"Ah." Okay, now I get it. "So who is she, then?"

"Aw, ma."

"A mother always knows. So, tell me."

He exhaled a breath while rolling his eyes. "You aren't gonna like this."

"What, did you go and marry a stripper?"

He laughed, but then took another breath before he answered me. "It's Ellie Burlick."

I couldn't help but gasp. Of all the girls, in all of Australia… "From last year? The sister of the girl who died here? The one who was staying in my Inn? That Ellie Burlick?"

He nods, once. "See why I didn't want anyone to know?"

More fallout from the deaths Alec Beaudoin had caused. Ellie's sister had been one of the victims. Poor girl. When Ellie came into town to find out why her sister had died, she and Kevin had gotten pretty close. I just hadn't realized how close. Until now.

If it got out that Kevin was dating the sister of a victim in a case where he'd made the arrest, it would cast a shadow of doubt on the whole case. It would screw up the prosecution of the murderer Alec Beaudoin, cast suspicion on why Kevin made the arrest, make the Lakeshore police department look like a bunch of hicks…

And all Kevin had been worried about was letting his mom know he'd had an overnight guest.

Reaching behind myself, I picked up a random stack of papers and slapped Kevin across his chest with them.

"Hey," he said, "what was that for?"

"You go out there right now and you tell Cutter who you were with! You get that nice woman to vouch for you, and stick it up Cutter's pompous…nose," I finished, realizing just how loud my voice was becoming.

"Think he'll back down even then?" He rubbed at his chest like a big baby. A big, six-foot-tall baby. "I mean, he's my boss but he's not the brightest bulb in the box. He's a real drongo. If he thinks he can discredit me by dragging Ellie down too, I'm thinking that's where he'll aim his spear."

I hop off the desk and hug him again. I love my son. A mother never was so proud. "You dug yourself into this hole. Go dig yourself out."

"Thanks Mom," he said. "Been a long time since you had to give me advice."

"No it hasn't. You just don't notice all the times I tell you what to do. I'm too good at it."

He stepped back from me and his face became serious. "You didn't come here just to tell me how to be an upstanding bloke, did you?"

"No. I didn't. Although I'm glad I was here to smack some sense into you. Did you find enough to get a search warrant?"

"I think so." His frown was sour. "Thing is, Cutter won't go for it."

Cutter. The rock sticking up in the middle of the cattle path. Blocking everything.

Well. Like I've been saying, Lakeshore is a small town.

"You stay here," I say to him. "You tell Cutter exactly what you did…well, exactly where you were, anyway. You tell him. Give him no reason to push this idiotic arrest."

"Um, okay. Care to tell me what you'll be doing?"

"No." I shake my head, and put a finger up to my lips. "Better you don't know."

After another hug I leave him there in Cutter's office. On my way out, I give the Lakeshore Senior Sergeant of police a hard stare.

I sincerely hope it's the last time I see him standing there in that uniform.

He doesn't deserve it.

Back near the middle of town, just down the street from the fountain with its miserable little gurgle of water, is a plain white house a lot like every other white house next to it. I haven't been here much. Just once or twice. The couple who live here, the Browns, are nice folks. We say hello on the street. Everyone knows me, of course, because of my Inn.

Everyone knows the Browns, too, for a very different reason.

I knock on the door and wait, tugging at my unicorn necklace. No reason to knock again. The Browns are old but they aren't hard of hearing. Mrs. Mabel Brown greets me with a smile just a moment later. "G'day, Dell. Percy and I are just sitting down for a bit of a bite. Care to join us?"

"No, thanks Mabel. Can I pull Percy away for just a few minutes?"

"Well, I've made a mint pea salad and grilled chicken, but I'm sure he can give ya some time. Percy!" she called out, walking back into the house. "We've company, dear."

I stood in the living room, looking at the pictures of the Brown's grandkids on the wall, until Percy came out of the kitchen, walking slowly, shuffling his feet, his browned and weathered face smiling. "Why, Dell Powers. Always glad to see that mug of yers. What brings ya to our home tonight?"

"Mayor Brown," I greet him, "I need to talk to you about Senior Sergeant Cutter."

He made an impolite sound between his lips. "That man again. What's he done now?"

See? Everyone knows everyone in a small town.

It's all in who you talk to.

CHAPTER SIX

The Inn seemed so cold the next morning.

After talking to Mayor Brown and making sure he understood the issue with Cutter, it had been late. The sun had been setting on the Tasmanian wilderness, painting the green pines with hues of purple shadows. Lakeshore was rolling itself up for the night. The eastern sky was turning a deep indigo. I loved this time of the evening. Like a bridge between today and tomorrow, you know? It made me feel better, knowing a new day was coming.

I felt better after talking to the Mayor, too.

"I'm not able to get rid of him, ya know, but I do know someone that I can talk to." Percy had explained with a thoughtful shake of his head. "Been Senior Sergeant for years now. Gonna be hard to convince the folks that need convincing to remove him. Course, can't let him go arresting folks like your son just 'cause he's a mind to. I'll talk to him, don't know how much good it'll do but I'll fix it if I can, Dell. Ya have my word on it."

That might help fix part of the problem if he could pull it off. I was still going to make it my goal in life to see to it that Cutter lost his job anyway. That could wait for now, as long as I knew my Kevin was out of danger.

So it was well after the dinner hour when I got back to the Pine Lake Inn, and when I went looking for Rosie it was too late. My business partner had already gone home for the night. It was only a ten minute walk from the Inn to where Rosie and her hubby lived, but I just didn't have the energy to go back out. I was drained past the point of empty.

After making sure our night manager had things taken care of I made my way upstairs. I was heading to my room but to get there, I had to go past the room that Jess had been staying in. The stairs to the third floor are on the other end of the second floor hallway. No getting around it.

The officer was gone now. The coroner would have come and gone by now, and Jess with him.

But standing there outside of her room, I couldn't help but feel her presence, like she was still here, just waiting to pop out and say g'day.

Wishful thinking. My friend was gone. I would never see her again.

Forcing myself to look away I climbed up the stairs to my room. Once there I sank into my bed without even bothering to change out of the clothes I was wearing. Then I promptly cried myself to sleep.

The next morning was when the feeling of cold struck me. The Inn felt different. I knew it was just my mind coloring things, but I swear to you the place felt cold. Like all the negative feelings of yesterday had soaked the warmth out of the air.

Silly of me, I know, but sometimes you just can't help the way you feel.

I was up early, and down at the front desk before my usual time. Life at the Inn always starts early in the morning but today I was up before the sun. Rosie wouldn't be in for an hour or better yet. I busied myself with paperwork, and doing a bit of cleaning, and other little tasks. When the phone rang I jumped to answer, hoping it would give me a distraction, but it was the same glitch we can't seem to get rid of. Just static. No one on the line.

Death in Room 7

I checked the clock on the wall. I know I'm fond of saying time moves on but in this case it actually had. After seven o'clock now. I know our morning kitchen staff will have cooked up eggs and sausage and what-not, maybe even some pikelets if they've been industrious, but it's odd that Rosie isn't here yet.

Both of our work schedules are pretty fluid. Rosie is here for serving times and when special dishes need to be cooked but otherwise she comes and goes as she pleases. I literally live here, so twelve and thirteen hour work days just mean I'm working from home. I don't expect Rosie to be here as much as I am, but still…

I lost a good friend yesterday. One I hadn't seen in years. Maybe that was making me jumpy. Maybe that cold feeling that was still lingering was trying to tell me something.

There's one way to find out. I reach for the phone to call her.

Just as it rings again.

Startled, I jump back a step, clutching my hand to my chest as if the phone had been about to bite me. I take a breath, and calm down, and try again. With a quick look around to make sure no one saw me getting freaked out by a telephone, I grab the receiver up to my ear. "G'day, Pine Lake Inn."

"Morning, Mom."

"Hiya, Kevin. Glad to hear your voice."

"Are you now? Why's that?"

"It's, uh, no reason. Just happy it's you, is all." Because the phone was going to eat me. Because Rosie is missing and my friend is dead and I need to hear from a living person not a phone call full of static and white noise and half whispered words. That's what I wanted to say. "No reason at all."

"Oh. See, I thought it might've had something to do with a call Senior Sergeant Cutter got from Mayor Brown. Had the Senior Sergeant as mad as a cut snake. Basically screamed at me in the office for an hour then told me to get out. Even sent my search warrant over to the judge to be signed off on."

The search warrant for Horace's things. So we could find the key on him and prove what he'd done to Jess. I wondered what Mayor Brown had on Cutter that had gotten such quick results and then decided that I didn't really want to know, I was just glad that he did. "Do you think he'll still have it?" I ask in a hushed whisper.

"Don't know. Worth trying, I think. I'm going over to the judge's place now. Just thought ya might want to know."

"Thanks, Kevin. Keep me informed?"

"Will do. Mom...are you all right?"

He's such a good son. Here I was trying to hide my tangled knot of emotions and he saw right through me. "I've been waiting for Rosie to come in. She's not here yet and I'm—"

The front door opened and in came Rosie, dressed in a pink blouse and a purple skirt that I'm very certain were never meant to be worn together. Her hair had been hastily thrown up in a bun, as well. She smiled apologetically, but didn't race to the kitchen like I thought she would. Instead she stood there, waiting for me to be done with my call.

"Actually, she's here now," I told Kevin. "Just me being silly after all."

"Okay. If you're sure that's all it was." He doesn't sound convinced, but he doesn't push. "I'll be over as soon as this search warrant is signed."

"Over here? Why?"

"I thought you knew? Rosie gave Horace a room at the Inn. He's staying there until Jess's body gets released by the Coronial Court up in Hobart."

No, I did not know that. "Oh, right. Sure. Anyway, Kevin. It was good to hear your voice."

"Heh. Love ya too, Mom."

When he hangs up, I do too, locking eyes with my friend and business partner. "You gave Horace a room? Here?"

She wrapped her hands together, nervously playing with her fingers. "Yes, I did. I should've left a note, I know. Figured it was the least we could do, ya know? Jess dead, in our Inn?"

Which was good business sense, and it would make him easy to find once the search warrant was signed, but I really didn't want that man within a hundred miles of me.

That's when it hits me. I haven't told any of this to Rosie yet. Cutter left here thinking it was suicide—until my Kevin showed him different and he tried to use it against him—and Rosie left before I could talk to her, and now I was left with having to explain to her the things me and Kevin had found out.

So I took a deep breath, and began.

It was a much shorter story than I thought it would be. How could such an evil deed be summed up in just a few minutes?

"I...can't believe it." Rosie's blew out her cheeks and stared off into the middle distance behind me. "You think she was murdered? By who?"

"That's what I'm hoping Kevin can find out. This morning, actually."

"You don't think Horace...?"

"I don't know." Which was a lie, actually. Not that I wanted to lie to Rosie. It was just that what I knew and what I could prove at that point were two very different things. I did know it was Horace. I was certain of it. Just needed Kevin with that search warrant, and then we could prove it.

"Oh, Dell, I'm so sorry. I never would have let him stay here if I'd known!"

"Don't worry about it, Rosie. I suppose it was the right thing to do, given the circumstances," I had to admit. "Especially considering how you felt about Jess."

"Yeah," she muttered, dropping her eyes as she came around to the other side of the registration desk. "Truth be told, Dell, that's one of the reasons why I'm so late. I was procrastinating. I know I have to tell ya this part but it's going to be tough to say, straight out."

"What is it, Rosie?" Her secret, I realized. That thing she wanted to tell me about Jess. "You've been acting a bit odd ever since we found out Jess was coming here."

Rosie smoothed one hand across the desk and picked at wrinkles in her shirt with the other. "It's nothing I'm proud of knowing, mind you."

"Something about Jess?"

Rosie nodded, her face serious. "Back in Uni, Jess had this…job she worked."

"Sure, Rosie, we all did. We had to find our spending cash somewhere."

"I know. Thing is, Jess's job was a bit, um, less respectable than most."

"How d'ya mean?" I knew Jess as well as anyone back in those days. I mean, sure, she had her secrets. What girl doesn't at that age? She was one of my best friends, though. As good a friend as Rosie, in her own way, and a person just doesn't find people like that every day. I thought I knew all the important things there were to know about Jessica Sapp.

Now Rosie rolled her eyes to the side and chewed on the inside of her cheek before she could bring herself to tell me about this secret life Jess had apparently been living.

"Thing is, I never wanted to tell you about this, Dell. It was Jess's secret to keep or to give. But now, maybe it makes a difference.

Besides, it's not like it can hurt her where she's gone. Jess used to make a living as a, well, as a prostitute."

I was staring at her, I knew I was, but I was waiting for a punchline that never came. "Jess traded sex for money? While we were at University?"

"Started before that, near as I could tell. But, yeah, it went on while we were all friends back then. Until she took up with Horace. Then she stopped. I think. I'm sure she didn't do that sort of thing after they were together for keeps. Messed up as their relationship was, she loved him. I'm sure she would never do anything to hurt him."

"I'm not so sure he shared that feeling," I muttered. Rosie didn't argue.

So. Jess had been a prostitute in her younger years. Not the sort of thing a woman likes to hear about a good friend, but still. "It's not illegal here in the merry old land of Oz. Up in Sydney there's a whole industry. Government regulation and the like."

She nodded along with every word. "I know, but you heard the news stories a few years back from the Attorney General's office. There's a big concern that regulating that particular, um, industry only brings in organized crime and other baddies. And I tell you what, I used to see Jess with some real unsavory types."

I did remember the news stories. The Federal government was worried that Australia would be inviting the same kind of trouble on itself that Las Vegas did over in the States. Make prostitution a regulated enterprise and the mob will come with it. Not that Australia really had a mob, to speak of, but the idea had proven right more often than not.

And Jess had been doing that kind of work while I knew her. I never even imagined. I mean, I know she seemed to have a different boyfriend every week. Sometimes every night. Still, my brain refused to believe what Rosie was saying. "Are you sure?"

Again, Rosie just gave me a nod. "That's where she got all that money to flash around. Now, I know it's not illegal or anything but I'm just an old fashioned woman, Dell. I was just so mortified to know how it was with her. It never sat right with me."

Truthfully it sort of set my teeth on edge, too, but it was a woman's right to choose her own life. I wouldn't hold it against Jess. It was just one more piece of the puzzle to fit in.

Kevin had been right when he said I liked puzzles. I just never imagined one like this would ever come my way.

Could Jess's old life be catching up to her? Worse, could it be that she'd gone back to that lifestyle? Trading sex for cash could earn a woman who looked like Jess a tidy sum.

My line of reasoning came to its obvious conclusion.

If Jess was prostituting herself again, and Horace found out about it, that would give him one banger of a motive for killing her.

"Rosie, do me a favor?" As I step around the desk I take her by both arms. "This is important. Do you think you might take today off?"

"What? Dell, I'm sorry if I upset you, but—"

"No, I promise it was nothing like that. Thank you, for telling me. I needed to know. Someone killed her. There are no secrets now. I just want you home today. Somewhere that you'll be, um, safe."

"Safe?" Rosie's eyes can get pretty big when she's surprised. "Dell, what are you on about? It don't matter if we've got the Devil himself upstairs, I've got that roast to fix for lunch and don't even get me started on the dinner menu!"

"I know, I know, but you've got people who can handle that. Look. My son's coming over soon with a search warrant for Horace's room and effects. I don't want you to be here when that happens. If anything happened to you…"

Like Jess, is what I couldn't make myself say.

Death in Room 7

Rosie figured out what I meant anyway. She's always been able to understand me, whether or not I've actually said anything. "Sure, Dell. I've got some things piling up back at the house, anyway. And my man and me are still trying to…you know. Tell you what. I'll go make things straight with the serving staff and then take off. You can call me when things are settled here."

Relieved, I hug her tightly, glad there's one less thing I'll have to worry about. "Thank you. And thanks for telling me all of that. Really."

"But if he does turn out to be the Devil himself, you'd best call me first."

The way she says it makes me laugh, and maybe makes me feel a bit better.

"You'll be okay?" she asks me.

What can I do but shrug?

As Rosie makes off toward the kitchen, the phone rings again. Sure, why not? I needed one more thing to do. Reaching over the counter I pick it up. It's an internal call, the red light on the phone blinking twice, then going dark, then blinking twice again in a repeated pattern. A call from one of the rooms.

"Front desk, may I help you?"

Silence on the other end.

"Oh, don't tell me we've got more problems with the phones," I mutter to myself. "Hello? Is there anyone there? Can you hear me?"

A hideous burst of static nearly deafens me in that ear. I jerked the phone away to stare down at it, wondering if maybe we have moisture in the lines or mice chewing on the cables.

"The phones again?" Rosie asks, on her way out through the lobby.

I hold the receiver out to the end of its coiled cord for her to hear. She rolls her eyes, but gives me a serious look before she leaves.

I know if I don't call her soon she'll be calling me instead, to find out if I'm all right. At least, she'll call if the phones start working properly.

The static cuts out. A voice whispers, *"You don't know him."*

I think.

It might have been something else because I've got the receiver held out far enough that I can't really hear whoever is speaking. "Hello?" I ask, putting it back to my ear gently. "Hello, are you there?"

"Who's that, Mom?"

Kevin walked in while I was standing there talking to a disconnected line. Hopefully whichever guest had been calling will ring back in a few minutes.

I hung up, hoping that was all it was.

In the meantime I was much more interested in the piece of paper that my son was holding in his hand. Two other officers are with him, which makes half of the entire police force. I know the one, Maxwell Stocker. The other's face is familiar but I don't have a name to go with it. Newbie, must be.

"Nobody," I tell Kevin. "Phones are still buggy. That the warrant?"

"Yep. Your guest still up in his room?"

"Far as I know."

A shadow passed over the stairs. Me and Kevin and the two other officers turned as one to look.

Mister Brewster stood there, halfway down, one hand on the railing, dressed all in black. His oddly colored eyes regarded each of us. "Horace Sapp is still upstairs," he said, as if Kevin's question had been directed to him.

Then he made his way down the rest of the steps and turned toward the common room without another look at any of us.

"Now, who was that?" Kevin asked me.

"Mister Brewster. Stays with us at the Inn at various times of the year."

Death in Room 7

Kevin keeps watching Mister Brewster for a moment, through the door to the common room, then shrugs one shoulder. "Odd man."

"More than most." There's really no way to put a description to Mister Brewster. I've given up trying. With a quick glance at the registration book I find the room number that Rosie had put Horace into. "It's the room right next to where Jess was. Come on. I'll show you."

"I'd rather you stayed down here," Kevin told me, that look on his face that says he needs to protect me. Big tough police officer watching out for his mother.

Which means…

"You found something out, didn't you? Something about this case?"

"Mom, you know I can't tell you things like that."

"You just did." He might think he needs to protect me, but I'm one smart lady. "Must be pretty serious. I just spoke with you this morning. What could you find out between then and now?"

He knew I had him. No sense in trying to deny what was written all over his face. Still, he can't just blurt things out to his mother on an ongoing investigation. I get that. Looking behind him at Maxwell and the other guy, he takes me by the elbow and ushers me over to the other side of the room.

"Mom, you know I can't tell you anything," he says, loud enough for the other officers to hear.

Then he lowers his voice to a whisper.

My kid's a smart one.

"We traced the numbers on her mobile. Lot of the usual. Her husband, her mother, a few friends. Then there was a bunch of calls to and from another number. Traced that to a woman by the name of Torey Walters."

I searched my memory. "I don't know that name."

"No reason you should. She's a prostitute. Not sure why Jess would have her in her contact list. Might just be a friend. Thing is, I recognized the name right off."

I'm sure my expression said it all.

"Not like that, Mom, seriously." With his face turning red, he rolled his eyes. "Like I already said, me and Ellie have a thing going. I've got no reason to go anywhere else."

That might be more than I needed to know, but in a strange way it was nice to hear. Besides. I'd started it.

"Anyway," he whispered, intentionally bringing the conversation back to Jess and this prostitute, Torey. "I recognized the name from the Roy Fittimer case. Remember our famous drug dealer? She was a known associate of his, suspected of helping him run his product. The Australian Federal Police were supposed to be working on that angle. Haven't heard anything since."

"Why? What are they dragging their heels for?"

"Might have something to do with a piece of information that was almost buried in the report. Roy had connections to organized crime. He was an up and coming drug dealer, he was. Got himself noticed by the heavy bad guys. Which means this Torey had those same connections, too."

I sucked in a breath. Rosie's words came back to me. Prostitution and organized crime. Jess's past might have more to do with her fate than even she had realized.

"So," he says to me slowly, letting me process all this information. "Do you have any idea why your friend would have been calling this Torey Walters?"

Unfortunately, yes I did. If he'd asked me that question yesterday, or even just a few hours ago, I would have said no. There was no way Jess would associate with that kind. Prostitutes. Drug dealers. Organized thugs.

Did I even know my friend at all?

As I tell Kevin all the sordid details as Rosie gave them to me, I could see things adding up behind his eyes. He was coming to the same conclusions as I had, no doubt about it.

"That puts things in a new light," is his comment. He's talking to me like a cop now, and I try not to take offense. "She might have been slipping back into her old ways. Her and Horace had been having trouble. Maybe she wanted to find comfort in the old familiar, and make some money on it besides. Or maybe she was even coming down to Lakeshore to see if she could pick up the pieces of Roy's drug business. I don't know. I do know this. If Horace knew that she was making these calls to Torey…"

"It would be the perfect motive for murder," I finish for him. "Right. Already landed on that myself."

He puts his hand on mine, and now there really is comfort in his protecting me.

With a nod, he tells me that's all he knows. For now it's back to the show.

"Now, I don't want to say it again," Kevin says in his normal voice, stepping back from me, nodding to the two officers like he's just put me in my place. "I just can't tell you anything, Mom. It's just the way of it. Be against Cutter's explicit orders."

Right. I keep the smile from my face and act all upset like I've just had the talking to of my life.

After all, we sure wouldn't want to go against Senior Sergeant Cutter's explicit orders.

Sometimes, sarcasm helps.

Don't you think?

CHAPTER SEVEN

I've never spent such a long half hour in all my life.

That's how long, according to the clock on the wall, that Kevin was upstairs with Horace. I must've paced a little trench right through the floor with all that walking back and forth. When one of the guests asked me what we were serving for dinner I'm pretty sure I told her we were serving water. She walked away with a confused look on her face, anyway.

When another guest asked what all the noise was upstairs I just said the police were handling it.

My little Inn was getting quite the reputation. Maybe I should just have Cutter set up his office in the lobby.

That reminded me. I picked up the phone and dialed quickly. With just a few words, I kept my promise to a friend.

When they finally came back downstairs, it was with Horace in handcuffs. His stringy hair was all over the place and his face was beet red. And he wouldn't shut up.

"I didn't do this! Are you insane! Why would I kill me wife? Why? Why!"

Maxwell and the other officer took him out, still struggling and arguing, to the waiting police car in the parking lot. The Lakeshore PD had exactly two police cars at the moment. I saw that they'd brought the better one for this. The one that didn't have rust all up around the front fender.

When the front door closed behind them, Kevin broke into a smile and held up a plastic evidence bag.

Inside it was the missing key.

There we go Jess, I said to her in my thoughts. We got him. We'll make him pay.

"Wasn't even hidden very well," Kevin said. "You'd think after being here two days he would have done something more'n just stuff it in the trash bin."

"That's where it was?" I can't believe that, either. Definitely not a criminal mastermind. Just a murderer. "Well, no one ever said Horace was the smart one. Doubt that Jess took up with him for his brains."

I took another, closer look at the key, just to make sure it's the same one we were missing. "What's that?"

Stuck to the key is a colorful pink square of waxed paper. Looks familiar, somehow.

"Candy wrapper," Kevin explained, turning the bag round to look at it himself. "Some kind of hard candy. Was stuck to the thing when we found it. Lots of others in the trash, too. Guess our Horace has a bit of a sweet tooth."

Huh. "Not something you picture a murderer doing, right? Sucking on candies while he…while he plans to…"

I can't make myself even say it.

Kevin put the key in its bag into his pocket. "No, I suppose not. Some killers have been caught by having a smoke and leaving behind the butt end of a cigarette. Guess this guy doesn't smoke."

Thinking back to University, I believe Kevin's right. I don't ever remember seeing Horace have a smoke. Or Jess, for that matter.

Don't remember Horace being much of a candy fiend, either, but I suppose he had to do something while he waited to kill my friend.

"So he got here early, killed Jess, then left again. Just like you thought."

"Right. Then came back in all vinegar and bluster to make it look like he had just shown up. Pretty crafty, I guess. Just not crafty enough. We'll know the answers to all the other little bits when the Coroner's done their investigation."

It all fit together. It just seemed, I don't know, too easy. Killer in our midst, killer caught, killer arrested. All because he threw the most incriminating piece of evidence in the trash along with his candy wrappers. Not exactly movie of the week material.

"Mom," Kevin said, with a shake of his head. "I know that look. Ya have to let this go. Your friend got killed. Right here in your Inn. You're gonna feel some guilt over that. Don't let it make you crazy. We got him. The bugger won't be getting away with it. Spend most of the rest of his life in prison, I'd wager."

I like the way that sounds.

"Didn't Cutter want to be here to show off?" I asked him. "Figured he'd be mugging for the cameras on this one."

"Heh." He scratched a finger behind his ear. "Yeah. Don't think Cutter's going to be sticking his face in public anytime soon. Still not sure what you did, but I'm grateful."

"Hey. A mother will do anything for her son. You'll find that out yourself one day."

"Subtle, Mom. Kids aren't on my horizon just yet. Me and Ellie are just starting out, and I don't want to put that kind of pressure on her."

I pull him to me, and kiss his cheek. "I know that. Take your time, son. Find the right one. If it's Ellie, make her happy. Just make sure you pick the right one."

My voice is tight with emotion. Kevin sees right through it.

"It's not your fault that dad left us."

"I don't know that," I tell him. "He never told me why he left."

His smile tried for reassuring but fell just a bit short. "He left us, Mom. Left us both. He had his own reasons. Might not know what those were, but I know it wasn't because of you. He loved you. Lots of things in life I might hold a doubt on, but that ain't one."

When I continue to doubt him, he tells me one more time. "Dad loved you. Whatever made him leave, it was something besides you."

I wish I could believe him.

∽

I was walking the halls of the Inn. It was night. Under my robe I was in my pajamas, the striped ones with the girlie butterflies up the front of the shirt on the right side. I wasn't even really sure why I left my bed. I'd been warm and comfortable there and in spite of the emotionally jarring events of the past few days—or maybe even because of them—I'd fallen asleep quickly.

When I stood in front of the room Jess had been staying in, staring at the door, I knew this had been my destination all along. I needed to see the room again.

The maids had been told to leave the room alone, for now, in case the police needed to go over the murder scene again. It would be just like it had been two days ago, only without Jess's body.

Thank God for small blessings.

I take the key for the door from my robe. It has candy wrappers stuck to it. I shake them off, and they fall away to the floor at my feet.

The door is open when I turn back to it. Inside, the room has been made spotless with the floors cleaned, the bed made up, all ready for the next guest…except for the bloodstain that formed its irregular pattern on the rug. Little droplets, tiny and scattered, still lead away from the chair to the window.

"Sorry about the mess," Jess says to me. "Didn't have time to clean up for ya."

I could weep, I'm so happy to see her. In those ripped jeans and that Grateful Dead t-shirt, her blonde hair all swept back into a clip, she's more the Jess I remember from Uni. "You're all right!" I blubber, even though I know that's not true. She can't be alive. I saw her, dead, here in this very room.

"It's a lot to explain," she says to me, smiling, turning…

As she turns, her clothes change. One moment, she's in a college girl's Friday night outfit. The next, she's in a slinky black dress. High heels with straps around the ankles. Dark panty hose. Her hair changes, too, into a carefully prepped and curled style, back to the black dye job from when she checked in.

She winked at me, and blew me a kiss with painted lips.

An escort's outfit. This is what a woman would wear to go out and about with a man on her arm.

"I made good money at it," she says to me, spinning in place with her hands above her head, luxuriating in this new look. Then she stopped, and her eyes snapped open in my direction. "Don't judge me."

"I'm not," I promised, although in my mind that was exactly what I'd been doing. I was putting myself in her place, thinking how I would have made different choices. I never would have put myself out like that.

So to speak.

Jess ran both hands down her sides, over the dress, and sighs. I can feel the reluctance in her silence as she turns sideways again, into her jeans and t-shift and blonde hair. It was like she had been more comfortable in the black dress. Like she missed having that part of her life.

And like she hated having to hide it from me.

She walked away from me, to the window. Even though I know how late it is, deep in the night, the sun is shining outside, silhouetting my friend's girlish figure.

"Jess…" I started to explain myself, to tell her it was all right, to ask her to please not be dead.

Bent down over the window, like she was staring outside at the ground, she held up her finger. Crooking it at me in a come-here sort of way, she said, "Look."

Without seeming to move I'm at the window standing beside her. She didn't turn to me. She didn't speak. She just stared out the window. Following the direction of her gaze, down, I realize that it isn't the grass or the edge of the crystal blue lake she's looking at. It's the windowsill.

The blood spatter traces up the wall, to the edge of the window, had been interesting enough. That had been our first clue that this wasn't a suicide. Someone who killed herself isn't going to walk to the window while her wrists are bleeding. Not without getting blood everywhere. Not without making a return trail. This one went to the window, and then stopped.

Even more interesting than that is what Jess was showing me now on the other side of the windowsill. A footprint. A man's boot. Clear as day, there in the midnight sun.

Outlined in blood.

"You don't know him," Jess says to me, standing there now with her arms folded and a smirk curling her lips.

Those words. I remember those words. From the phone call. I hadn't been sure if I'd really even heard them at all.

I was sure now.

Jess had been trying to reach me. Well, her ghost had been trying to reach me, anyway. Her spirit. To tell me something. To tell me…what?

That I didn't know him.

Which was when my brain finally accepted the fact that Jess was dead and none of this was real and even though it felt so good to have my friend standing right there, right here with me and close enough to touch, I would never have that again.

I woke up in bed, sitting bolt upright, gagging on a breath and shaking in the tangle of sheets. The dream had been so vivid. I felt over both shoulders, just to make sure I wasn't actually wearing a robe with a key in it that was plastered with little candy wrappers. I wasn't. Just the purple pajamas with the butterflies on them.

Trembling, I reached over to the lamp on the bedside table and switched it on. The clock read four thirty-eight in the morning. I could get maybe another two hours of sleep before I would have to get up and attend to the Inn. Somehow, I was pretty sure I wouldn't get back to sleep if I tried.

The thing was, I knew that dream was more than just a dream. That hadn't been some memory of Jess, or my subconscious making up a version of my friend for me to talk to. That had been Jess. Her ghost. Spirit? Soul, maybe. I wasn't clear on the right lingo. Talking with ghosts wasn't exactly something I did on a regular basis.

But I knew someone who did.

Jess's words weighed heavy on me as I found the number I wanted, tucked into the contact list in my mobile. "You don't know him," she'd said. I was beginning to believe that. Horace wasn't the man I remembered from back in Uni. I certainly didn't like the man back then, not very much, but I would've never guessed he was capable of murder.

I used the Inn's phone to dial. It was going to cost me either way, but less so if I used the landline. I messed up the first try and had to hang up and dial again. American phone numbers were weird. Too long.

The phone on the other end rings, and a woman's voice answers. "Hello?"

"Hi. Um. It's Dell Powers. From Australia. Sorry, I know it's early. Did I wake you?"

"No, Dell. It's just in the afternoon here. Two-thirtyish. Different time zones, remember?"

"Right, right." Of course. I'm on the other side of the world. "So, um, the reason I called. I kind of need your help."

"Anything Dell. Although I'm not sure what I can do for you from America."

"Need your advice. You sure I'm not bothering you?"

I could hear her talking to her husband away from the phone for just a moment, and then I was sure I heard a cat meow before she got back on the call with me. "No bother at all. Jon was just leaving to go back to work. We had a late lunch together. So I'm all yours. Tell me what's going on."

After a deep breath, I pushed myself to say it. Out loud. "My dead friend. Her ghost. I think. I mean, I think I was just talking to her ghost. In a dream. I know this all sounds totally crazy. It was just so real." I make myself slow down. "You've got all the experience in this sort of thing, right? Leastwise, from what you told me on your honeymoon, you do."

There was a pause, a moment in time when I was sure she was going to tell me that I really was crazy and this isn't how these things go and just go back to sleep and don't worry about it.

Instead, I could almost hear her smiling. "Oh, Dell. You don't sound crazy at all. Believe me. And I'll tell you anything you need to know. Let's start from the beginning, okay?"

I let myself breathe again. It felt so good, knowing there was someone I could talk to who would understand. Someone who wouldn't think I was crazy. Nice to have friends, no matter where they live.

"Thank you, Darcy," I said to her. "This is what happened…"

CHAPTER EIGHT

After a talk with my friend Darcy Sweet I was left with more questions than answers. I felt better by the time I hung up, though. Darcy had explained the ins and outs of ghostly apparitions to me. Dreams were a common way for the deceased—but not necessarily departed—to communicate with the living. When you slept, she said, your mind's defenses lowered. You were more open to contact from the other side.

Jess had spoken to me in my sleep. The question became, what was she wanting to say to me?

Darcy didn't have an answer for me there. She said that part was up to me to figure out.

I was dressed and walking downstairs to start my day. With all these thoughts going through my head I was standing in the middle of the second floor before I realized it. The door to Jess's room was right beside me when I looked up. Just like it had been in my dream.

"*You don't know him.*" I hope to God that Jess has more to tell me sometime, because that wasn't much to go on. Kevin had her killer in custody. Her husband. Telling me I didn't know him was like telling me water was wet.

The rest of the dream played through my mind, mixed in with all my other jumbled thoughts. Maybe, if I went in to look, things would be like they were before and I'd see something that we had missed…

I put my hand to the doorknob. My fingers settled around the cold metal and I held them there while I tried to make myself believe I wasn't scared.

Then, in the next breath, I took my hand back. Maybe when the sun was up. Maybe that would be a better time. After all, the thing was done. I wouldn't gain anything by putting myself through that again. Doing it in my dream had been hard enough.

Downstairs I found a note from my night manager. She leaves at midnight. After that there's a sign we put out for the guests telling them to ring my room if they need something. As an Inn, that doesn't happen very often, thankfully. We're not one of those brand name hotels up in Hobart where people come and go at all hours.

The note says that Kevin was here, late last night, wanting to see me about something important. When Ann—my night manager—had told him I was already asleep he'd said it could wait until morning.

I smile at that. He's such a good boy. Wish he'd woken me, though. It had to be about Horace Sapp, and now I was burning with curiosity. Hopefully I could catch him at home.

I've known Kevin's number by heart for years. I have trouble remembering his cell phone but then that's what contact lists are for. I try his home phone first, and after two rings someone answers.

It's just not Kevin.

Instead, a familiar, deep female voice greeted me. "Hello?"

Hm. "Ellie Burlick. How are you?"

"Oh. Um. Hi, Dell. You probably wanted Kevin, I reckon?"

"I did. But I see I got you for the moment. How've you been?"

"Fine, thank you. Much better than the last time we spoke. Um. Kevin told ya I was here visiting, right?"

"He did. Not to worry, Ellie, I'm happy for him. He's needed a good woman in his life for a long while."

The relief in her voice is almost funny. "Too right. A bit rough around the edges, your son."

There's laughter on the other end, hers and Kevin's both. Then I hear the phone changing hands. "Hi, Mom," Kevin says. "I think I'll just take over the call from here."

"Oh, but Ellie and I were having so much fun."

"Sure." There's a short pause, and I imagine he's saying something to Ellie that he wouldn't want his mother to hear. "Okay. Mom, listen. We got the report from the Coronial Court late yesterday. There's things you should know."

Things? "Kevin, I don't understand all that technical lingo. I'm sure you can explain it all to the magistrate at the trial."

"That's the thing of it," he says to me. "May not be a trial."

"What? Kevin, he—" With a quick look around the room, I make sure none of the staff is close enough to hear me, and then lower my voice anyway. "He killed Jess. How is there not going to be a trial? Did he confess or something?"

"No, it's a lot more complicated than that. We should meet. At the Inn. Give me twenty minutes and I'll be over."

Rosie was at the Inn by the time Kevin arrived. Was it already Saturday? Hard to believe, with everything that had been going on. She and I spoke for a while about Jess, and Horace. It was the talk of the town by now, of course, helped along by the morning newspaper. James Callahan had written a full, front page article about the whole thing. The paper gets delivered early in Lakeshore, to every door that subscribes, my own included. I must say, he had some very good information.

Almost like someone who knew the facts had given him a phone call.

"Just can't believe it, even still," Rosie said to me. "Who would have thought this would be the way of it, back when we were in University?"

"I know." I'd been thinking a lot about the past myself. Guess my dream had put me in a mind for it. "Life goes on, though."

"Oh, that reminds me I've got to start the breakfast if'n we expect to have anything to serve! Dippy eggs don't make themselves!"

She turned, almost knocking over a cup filled with pens and pencils in her haste. Smiling, she righted the cup and backed away from the registration desk.

When she turned to go through the door to the kitchen she yelped and hopped on the foot she stubbed against the frame.

That was my Rosie. Awkward as if she were still a teenager. I doubt she'll ever outgrow that.

Nice to know there are some things that will never change.

Kevin was a little more than the twenty minutes he'd promised in getting here. Odd, considering his house is ten minutes away at best. I suppose he had things to attend to at home.

And good on him for that.

He's dressed in his uniform, dark blue shirt buttoned up tight, duty belt strapped on with his sidearm and his handcuffs. In his hand is a manila folder.

"It looks like you're dressed for work," I tell him. "You have time for some breakfast? I think Rosie's making puffed cheese omelets today."

"Seriously? The ones with the rosemary and sage?" I could tell he was considering it, but then he just shook his head. "Not now. I need to show you this first."

Raising the folder for me to see, he put it out flat on the registration desk between us. That's when I saw the white label on the tab.

"The report from the coroner?"

"Yup." He opened it up, the pages inside turned to face me. "It came by special courier late last night."

"I thought it was going to take a week or more?"

"Well, this is a preliminary report only. Maybe it's a slow week up in Hobart. Plus, we were able to tell them this was a murder, after Cutter got off his high horse, so they rushed it for us."

"Kevin, I told you I don't understand any of this." Half the words were in Latin or lawyer-speak, which is just about the same thing to me. "Should you even be showing this to me?"

He shrugged. "Way I see it, I'm conferring with a witness."

"Might want to add a translator into the mix. Why don't you break this down for me? What's in here that's so important?"

He flipped a page, then another, then started pointing to facts that still look like a meaningless jumble on the page to me. "Here's the part about the cuts to Jess's arms. To the naked eye they don't look that special. Closer examination showed the cuts weren't smooth. They were jagged inside. Most likely made by a serrated blade."

I can feel my eyes getting wider. "Jess had a razor blade in her hand. That doesn't have a serrated edge."

"Exactly my point. There's more." He stopped, looking up from the pages at me, his eyes full of concern. "Are you sure you want to hear this?"

No, was my first thought.

Yes. Maybe.

No?

"Yes, I do. I need to know what happened to her. I need to know that we got the man who killed her."

"Well, now, that's the meat of it." He flipped another page and scanned, upside down, until he found the right paragraph. "I'm only showing you this because she was your friend and, well, Cutter's probably gonna have my head if he finds out, but…here. The examination found a tiny pinprick, inside one of the cuts. Like a needle mark."

"Inside the cut?" I tried to picture it. The only way that could happen was if someone had intentionally poked a needle into one of the cuts, or…"You think someone injected her with something, then cut over the mark."

"Always knew I got my smarts from you, Mom." He turned a couple pages back. "In her body they found a high level of pentobarbitone. That's a sedative. Remember how we were wondering why Jess would just sit there and let someone kill her?"

"She was sedated." Horace had injected her with this pentobarbie thing. Jess hadn't fought back because she couldn't. "That low life. That sicko coward. Snuck into my Inn to drug my friend and then kill her. I can not believe—"

"Mom. I don't think it was him."

It was like a cold slap to hear him say it. "What? Kevin, didn't we already decide it was Horace? Everything fit. What is it you're always saying? Means, motive, opportunity!"

"Sure, all that. Except now we have the physical evidence."

"We found the key to Jess's room in his waste bin!" I reminded him. "It was him, Kevin!"

George the handyman walked into the room right then, with that stupid painting of Governor David Collins under his arm. He stopped, eyes wide, as he heard me yelling at Kevin. "Uh, I'll come back."

Then he turned and hurried in the other direction.

I sighed, scrubbing my face with my hand, and lowered my voice. "Kevin, Horace did this. Even the newspaper said so."

"Yeah, 'bout that." Kevin tapped a finger on the registration counter. "Strange how Callahan knew so much for that article of his.

Even had the bit about the search warrant. Almost like someone called him, or something. Wouldn't you say?"

I shrugged a shoulder, unable to meet his eyes. He obviously knew what I'd done. I didn't think I'd done anything wrong. I didn't say anything that Callahan wouldn't have heard for himself. Eventually. Plus, I'd promised.

"Anyway," Kevin went on. "There's enough here to make me rethink accusing Horace. That's what I wanted to tell you."

"Not sure I want to hear it." I folded my arms, wanting to forget any of this had ever happened. "It had to be him, Kevin. Someone had to get close enough to stick Jess with a needle. Who else could do that but someone she knew?"

"Okay, Mom, listen to me. Just hear me out. The cuts on Jess's arms weren't made by the razor blade. Fine, that helps prove it was murder. But then what? Follow the logic with me. Horace is dumb enough to leave the key to Jess's room in his waste bin, but where's the knife that made the cuts? Where's the needle? He remembered to get rid of those but left the key for us to find? Does that make any sense to you?"

I thought about it, turned it in my head every which way I could, until I was finally forced to agree with him. It didn't make sense. It didn't mean Horace wasn't the killer, far as I was concerned, but all those little things sure did cast their doubts. "So what happens now? Are you and Cutter just going to let Horace go?"

"No. He's still the only suspect we have. And this don't say he's innocent. Just enough to get me thinking. We'll hold him for now. Just need to do some more investigating. Can we go up to the room again?"

"You think you missed something?"

"No. I think Cutter might've, though. He did the search of the room."

Death in Room 7

Had to agree with him there. Cutter was pretty slack on his best day. Considering he hadn't even treated Jess's death as a crime scene at first, there was a fair to middling chance that if there was something to miss, then he missed it.

I sorted through the keys on my ring for the master key. The spare had gone in an evidence bag after the search of Horace's room. The other two had been bagged up with Jess's things. As I found the right key, I asked him, "Horace isn't your only suspect, right?"

"Eh? What do you mean?"

"This girl that Jess was calling. What's her name? She'd be a suspect too, wouldn't she?"

"Torey Walters. Right. Not exactly a suspect, but we're tracking her down. Seems she don't want to be found."

Well. Here I was set to start putting Jess's death behind me, with Horace arrested and behind bars. Guess the whole mess was a bit more twisted than all that. A big old ball of yarn. Every thread we pulled on drew out three or four others, all tangled up.

"Up to the room then," I say, trying for a smile and failing.

"It's alright," Kevin told me. "We'll figure this out. You and me."

Going up the stairs together we get to Jess's room without seeing anyone else. It's only now that I realize I've been calling this Jess's room, as if it would always be hers somehow. Room Seven. Jess's room.

I open the door wide and see her standing there.

In a blink, she's gone. Just the memory of her smiling at me remains. Kevin caught me as I jumped back, the hair at the back of my neck standing up. I held onto his arm to steady myself.

"Mom? You alright?"

"Uh. Yes. Sorry. Thought I saw something."

"Like a ghost?" he joked, walking past me into the room.

I don't answer him. That's kind of exactly what I just saw.

She'd been standing over by the window, in the same clothes I'd seen her wearing in my dream. Darcy had told me how ghosts are often tied down to the place where their death occurred. Sometimes they'll appear in places that had a significant meaning to them, like their home, or their place of work, or a favorite park. More often, it was where they died.

Maybe this was more Jess's room now than I had realized.

As Kevin began looking under the pillow on the bed, and under the mattress, and obvious places like that, I went to the window where I had seen Jess. I was very careful to walk around the blood stains from where she died, and the spatters of blood that led from there, along the floor, and up the wall to this window here. In the dream, Jess had shown me something outside while standing in this same spot, something that I was only just remembering.

And there it was. When I bent my head against the glass to look, I could see the partial imprint of a shoe on the windowsill, set into the spatters of blood that were still there.

The windows of my Inn all open outward, and there's a wide ledge on each. On the third floor the windows don't open at all. The insurance won't allow it. Down here on the second floor we've never had a problem with it. At least, not till now.

"Kevin, come look at this."

Dropping the mattress back into the frame, my son joined me at the window. He frowned when he saw what I was looking at. "You don't have fire escapes on the Inn, do you?"

"'Course we do. At either end of the second and third floors there's an emergency door that opens out to an emergency ladder bolted against the side of the building."

"But not on the windows."

"No. Not on the windows."

He turned his head sideways, trying to get a better angle to view the print. "Then why would our killer—Horace or whoever else—climb out the window after killing your friend?"

"We know he left the key in the next room." I didn't mention that was the room Horace had been in.

But it was.

"Right, sure, so he went from this room to the other, I get that. But why go out the window? Wouldn't he just walk down the hallway from here to there? I mean, what did he do, jump?"

I agree it sounded like a pretty stupid plan, as murder plots went. Horace kills his wife, then leaps from one window ledge to the next to get away instead of just strolling up the hallway past all the other guests...

Then the reason hit me in the face. "Oh, I know why. There's guests staying at the Inn. Even in the middle of the night, if Horace had left Jess's room after killing her he risked being seen."

"But jump from window to window," Kevin added, "and you can leave the door locked behind you and not a trace you were even there."

"Except for the blood he dripped to the window, and then stepped in."

"Probably dripped off the knife he used to kill her." He thought it through as we stepped out into the hallway and over to the other room. I got my key out as we went. "If he was here at night, with the lights off, he might not have even known he was leaving the trail. Or leaving prints. I'll have to get a picture of that. Maybe even an imprint lift."

In here, the place was still a mess from when the police had dragged Horace out. No way was I thinking of this as his room. The other one could be Jess's room, but no way would this ever be Horace's. I looked around, knowing I was going to have to get the place cleaned up so I could rent it out again.

Would I have to do that with Jess's room, I asked myself. Yes. I would. Eventually.

Just not today.

"Here it is," Kevin said, head pressed to the glass pane of the room's only window. "Not a footprint, but the edge of the sill is broke off. Like somebody landed on it bad."

"Okay." I brought myself back to the present and came over to see. Great. Something else for George to repair. "So he used the key to sneak into her room, killed her, jumped from window ledge to window ledge, and exited through here when no one was looking. That way no one would see him coming out of a dead girl's room."

"Amazing jump," is Kevin's comment. "How'd he get in on this side?"

I sigh, closing my eyes and pinching the bridge of my nose. "Easy enough. We keep the windows open in the rooms that aren't in use when it's hot. Keeps the place cooler."

Kevin lifts the curtain screen away from the window. It just hangs like a shade, simple enough and effective without being in a guest's way. Also made it easy for Jess's Killer to slip in and out.

I opened my eyes again to see Kevin looking at me with that police officer look that he gets sometimes.

"I know, I know," I told him, raising my hands in exasperation. "I need to beef up security at the Inn. How many times have you told me?"

"Not enough, apparently."

"Well, if I'd known my good friend was going to be murdered in the room next door then I would have changed the locks!"

"Mom, it's okay. It's not your fault."

My son held me as I fought back the tears. How I wish to God his father was here. I've missed that man of mine for so long I can't remember not missing him. And hating him, too, for leaving us. He was here for me when I started this Inn. Then, poof, just gone one day.

Well, he wasn't here for me now. Kevin was. He and I had a puzzle to put together. No sense crying over it.

Because, hey, life goes on. Whether we want it to or not.

"You really don't think Horace did this?" I asked him, pushing out of his embrace and wiping at my damp eyes with my fingertips.

I could tell he was gauging his answer, second-guessing himself for telling me any of this. Finally he shook his head, his eyes full of apology. "No, Mom. I don't think Horace did this. Too many things just ain't adding up anymore. I won't let him go until I'm sure, but I think someone else killed your friend."

There it is, then. I square my feet and set my jaw and meet this as straight on as I can. "So then, what are we going to do about it?"

"We? Mom, this is police business from here on out. I already told you too much. Kind of figured you needed to hear it, but I'm the police officer in the family."

"You're going to find this Torey Walters, aren't you?"

"Sure. 'Course I am. She's somewhere in Tasmania now. We're sure of that much. Probably find her before the day is over."

Well that was news. "How'd you figure out she was here in Tasmania?"

He smiled like he's got secrets his mother doesn't know. "I've got a friend working on it. Thanks for the help. Er, try not to let any more info slip out to the newspaper, right?"

I smile, because his mother actually does have secrets her son doesn't know about.

CHAPTER NINE

Saturdays in Lakeshore are just like Saturdays most everywhere else in Australia, I suppose.

The town becomes a lazy backdrop of people walking dogs and mowing lawns and just strolling the streets. 'Course, some folks still have to work. The Inn doesn't run itself, for instance. The police force is in the middle of a murder investigation—well, another murder investigation, I suppose I should say. Lakeshore's becoming just like Adelaide in South Australia.

Well. Hopefully not that bad.

I had taken an early lunch, letting Rosie know I was going into town and leaving the "Please request help from the staff" sign on the registration desk. Rosie hadn't said anything to me but I could tell from her expression that she understood how Jess's death was weighing on me. She was being a good friend, letting me have space when I needed it.

The fresh air off the lakes was sweet in my lungs. I could hear it rustling the pines all around. People smiled and waved a greeting to me in passing. Some of them, the ones who knew me better or who were just bigger snoops than the others, stopped me to ask about the murder in my Inn. I was polite enough, but I'm sure they all got the hint that I didn't want to talk about it. None of the conversations lasted long.

This was my own little walkabout, I suppose. Time to clear my head and think. Maybe something would occur to me that would put the whole mess into perspective and help me make sense out of the death of one of my oldest friends.

On Main Street, past the fountain, I suddenly found myself wandering by Jonas Albright's church. I'm not sure if I'd planned the route out or if my feet just took me where they thought I wanted to go. I'm not a churchgoer, mind you. My Catholicism lapsed years ago. Sometime around when my husband left me, actually. Maybe that wasn't God's fault. I just couldn't bring myself to face Him with so much anger in my heart.

But that was then, and this is now, as they say. Right now I could sort of use some spiritual guidance. Pastor Jonas Albright might just have an answer or two that I was missing.

The church was a one story building with a high peaked roof that was in need of repair. Shingles were loose in more than one spot. The soffit was loose around that one corner, and it probably hadn't seen a fresh coat of paint in five years or more. Lakeshore has only a small congregation. Hard to draw funds for repairs when there weren't that many hands giving.

A wooden cross made from crooked pine tree limbs was fixed above the front door. The place was simple and honest in its faith. I've always liked that about Pastor Albright. Not a lot of us here in Lakeshore make use of his sermons, but he still struggles on, ministering to those who want to hear and those who need to hear besides.

Which was what I was hoping he could do for me today.

Up the front steps I went and then quietly slipped in through the door. Not that there'd be big mobs of people inside to disturb. Services were on Sundays, which would be tomorrow, and today the house of worship was just another building open to the Lord above and the townsfolk down here on Earth.

Sure enough, there was just the one guy inside. An older man with gray hair combed straight back from the high forehead of his gaunt face, wearing a long black overcoat. A stout black cane was leaning up against the end of the pew where he was sitting. He ignored me. I didn't recognize him, which was unusual for our small little town. Maybe he was a friend of Pastor Albright's.

The inside of the church was better kept than the outside. Dark wood paneling everywhere and a worn but colorful red rug that covered every inch of the floor. The pews were lined up in two neat rows. They'd seen better days but they were polished to a shine. At the front of the church was a raised platform with a small altar and a lectern where the pastor gave his sermons.

Except for the door that led to a back room that was mostly storage, that was all there was to the church. Like I said, it was a simple place. Thing was, Pastor Albright wasn't here.

"Excuse me," I said to the man in the pew. "Sorry to interrupt you. I was wondering if you could tell me where the pastor is?"

The man turned to me, his eyebrows up. "Well now. That's quite the surprise."

I wasn't sure what he meant by that. This was a church, after all. "I was just hoping to talk to him. Is he around?"

The man regarded me for a moment before nodding with his head to the back room. "I think you'll find what you're looking for in there."

"Thank you. You aren't from around Lakeshore, are you?"

"Oh, but I am. Before your time, I'm sure."

"Well I wasn't raised here, but I've owned the Pine Lake Inn over on Fenlong Street for a long time now. I don't think I've seen you there?"

"No," he said to me. "I don't get out much. Name's Heeral Stone. Pleased to know ya."

"Likewise. I'm Dell Powers."

"Ah. Well, that would explain it then, wouldn't it?"

Why did I have the feeling this man wasn't having the same conversation with me that I was? "Explain what?"

He stood up, supporting himself with his cane while he stooped over the pew to pick up a short, flat-topped hat. Then he walked up the row toward me. "There was another Powers family in Lakeshore some long years ago."

"Distant rellies," I told him, although I didn't know much about that side of my family. "It was one of the reasons why I chose to own an Inn here."

Heeral was walking past me now, eyes unfocused, like he was looking into the past. "Long years ago," he repeated.

He wasn't quite to the door yet when I heard Pastor Albright calling to me from the front of the church. "Ah, g'day Dell. Was wondering if ya might be coming to see me."

I turned and greeted him with a wave. "Sorry to disturb you, Pastor. I came in to talk a spell but I got distracted with your friend here…"

When I turned back to Heeral, he was already gone. For a guy with a cane he sure moved quickly. "Well, anyway. Do you have a few minutes for me?"

"Of course," Pastor Albright said without hesitation. "I understand ya had a good friend die in your Inn. She was visiting?"

I shifted on my feet. News travels fast in a small town and I wasn't surprised that he'd heard about Jessica already. It was just hard to talk about it now, what with everything my Kevin and I had figured out.

He asked me if I wanted to sit down and I accepted gratefully. Not that the wooden pews were very comfortable, but sitting down with him made me feel less like I was confessing my sins and more like I was talking to a friend. We sat in the same pew, facing each other, and he waited patiently for me to begin.

Pastor Albright was a short and—some might say—scrawny specimen of a man. His dog collar was a bright white strip at the top of his black short-sleeved shirt. With those round glasses of his I've always thought he looked like an owl. Especially now that his hair was receding on top. He'd been there for me more than once when I needed his help, though, and there were a lot of folks in town that could say the same.

Without going into details I told him about me and Jess, about her coming to the Inn, and about how she'd been found dead in her room. There was nothing there that he couldn't have read in the papers, to be sure. After all, I hadn't come to unburden my soul or ask if Jess had made it to Heaven.

I had another question in mind entirely.

"She sounds like an interesting person, your friend."

Pastor Albright had listened to my stories of our days in University, interrupting with questions I didn't always want to answer. I'd left out the part I'd recently learned, about her being a prostitute. Legal or not, this didn't seem the time or the place to bring up that little bit.

"She was one of my best friends," I told him honestly. Then I took a deep breath. "I'm not entirely sure what to make of this, but I think maybe she's still here."

He reached out and patted my hand with his. "Yes. We often feel like the dearly departed are still with us, and it's the truth that they will be, so long as we keep them in our hearts."

"I suppose so, but this is more than that. I have this other friend. An American. Her name is Darcy Sweet and—"

"Ah, yes! I remember her." He seemed pleased to hear Darcy's name. "Nice girl. Her and her hubby stopped at the church just the once, when they were here during that awful mess with the poisons. How is she?"

"Fine. She's fine. I was just on the phone with her, actually, about Jess."

"Oh?"

"Yes." I took another deep breath. Now that I was at this point I felt foolish. "Do you believe in ghosts, Pastor Albright?"

He sat back in the pew suddenly, trying to disguise the motion by crossing his legs. "I…I'm not sure what ya mean by that. Um. Ghosts? Why ask about such silly things?"

"Er, well. What if it wasn't silly? What if…what if Jess is still here? Her spirit, I mean."

"Her ghost," he suggested in a flat tone.

"Yes." I could see from his reaction that the topic was not sitting well with him. Now I really did feel foolish. I had figured if anyone in town would know about ghosts, and what to do to help them, it would be Pastor Albright.

Darcy had told me ghosts were real. She'd even told me that Jess could very well be haunting my Inn now—my words, not hers—if she'd been killed. What she couldn't tell me from half a world away was if Jess was really here, or if I was imagining it because I wanted to believe Jess was still around in some form.

I'd had this crazy thought that Pastor Albright might be able to come with me back to the Inn and, I don't know…*sense* her ghost. Help me reach Jess's spirit and find out what had really happened to her.

That idea died pretty quickly when he stood up and began wiping his hands together vigorously as if he was washing himself clean of the conversation. "There are no such thingums as ghosts, Dell. When we die, we move on to God's judgment. Heaven. Hell. We can't stay here in the mortal plane when we die. We have to go to one place or the other."

"So…there's no such things as ghosts?"

His eyes rolled nervously to the front of the church, then back to me. "It's natural to want to keep our loved ones with us. And we do, in our hearts and our heads. Now, I might be just a simple apple eater and a backwoods preacher, but I reckon I know a few things. See, people believe what they want. It's like I was telling this young woman who came through a few days back. Torey, her name was. She was confused about so many things. The path is always clear, I told her, when you're looking hard enough—"

"Wait." Could it be? "Pastor Albright, you said this girl's name was Torey?"

"Well, yes, sure. Not all that odd for a young lady seeking answers to come here. I always recommend going to church when you're lost. You're here for the same reason, isn't that right?"

It sure was looking that way. I'd been looking for answers, and Jonas Albright seemed to have a very big one, even if he didn't know it. "This girl, Torey, was her last name Walters?"

"I'm sorry, I didn't get her last name. She was, uh, short. Very thin. Like she'd been sick. Long black hair. A tattoo of a snake on her left shoulder. I thought you might've seen her by now."

"Why would you think that?"

"Well, I sent her on to your Inn. She needed a place to stay and as much as I want to be the Good Samaritan the Lord asks us to be, I thought it might look, um, suspicious for a single man to take in a wandering young woman like that."

Torey Walters. The prostitute that Jess had been calling. If Torey was here, then Jess hadn't just come here to visit me, her old friend Dell Powers.

She'd come here to meet with Torey.

And then she'd been killed.

How did Horace fit into all of that?

The simple answer was he didn't. I refused to believe that. He must've known about Jess stealing his card, or meeting with friends from her old life, and gotten angry, and found himself some phenobarbie-whatsit, and…and…

"Dell?" Pastor Albright was watching me, waiting for me to say anything. Or breathe, I suppose. "Are you all right?"

I stood up, my mind racing faster than an emu being chased by wild dogs. "I'm not sure if I'm all right or not. I know more than I did when I came in. I guess that's a start."

He moved out of my way as I stepped out of the pew and into the aisle. I could be wrong, but I got the impression he was happy to see me go, and take my questions about ghosts and spirits with me. "Well. I'm happy I could help ya, Dell. Come any time."

"I'm glad I came in, too. Your friend told me I'd find what I needed here."

"Friend? Did I miss someone?"

"The older gent. With the cane?" My mind was already on finding Kevin. He had to know about this. Torey Walters had been here. Where was she now?

When I looked up the pastor was still staring at me. His face had gone pale, his eyes wide. "Pastor Albright? Jonas, what's wrong?"

He blinked, coming to himself and clearing his throat. "Nothing. Not a thing. The older gent with the cane. Yes. Well. I, uh, have to get back to writing my sermon. Take care, Dell."

Without waiting to see if I had anything else to say, he turned and went up to the altar, then through the door to the back room.

I wasn't sure what to make of that. Not that I had a lot of time to think about it just now. I had to find Kevin. Hopefully, he'd be down at the police station.

Tell you this, though. The look on Pastor Albright's face was like he'd seen a ghost of his own.

I know I'm supposed to be going back to the Inn. The place doesn't run itself and Rosie, bless her soul, is busy enough in the kitchen without trying to pick up my slack at the front desk.

But I think a little side trip to the police station is in order.

Although side trip doesn't really describe a walk from one end of town to the other.

It's more than an hour before noon, but I've skipped breakfast again and as my belly begins grumbling in protest I figure I'll need something to keep up my strength. It's going to be a long day. So when I got to the Milkbar I charged a soft drink and a few chocolate bars to the Inn's account. There's a few perks to owning my own business. Running a tab at most of the other businesses in town is definitely one of them.

No such thing as ghosts. The good pastor had seemed so sure. Or had he? I remembered the way he looked just before I'd gone, and the way he'd been all nervous to begin with over the whole subject. Maybe he didn't believe in ghosts, but at the same time, maybe his words were covering up what he really believed.

On the other hand, Darcy had been very sure about what she believed. Ghosts were a real part of my American friend's life. The dead could reach out to the living, encourage them, guide them, even ask for help.

I know what I had felt, dreaming about Jess. Maybe it was just a dream, maybe not. But I couldn't deny how real it felt.

My friend needed my help. I could figure out the rest of my life some other time.

The bottle of no-name cola was gone by the time I got to the other edge of town. Oliver Harris was outside his two stall garage up here, banging away at the motor of a little red coupe that had its hood propped up with a broom handle. He got a lot of business being right across from the police station. 'Course, being the only tow truck driver in town helped, too. He waved one massive, grease-stained hand at me before whacking away at the engine again with a long monkey wrench.

Oliver had never been the brightest in his family. A high school football injury had pretty much limited his choices in life. For all that, I've never seen him unhappy. Maybe I should ask him his secret someday.

I didn't so much march into the police station as I slunk in, hoping that Senior Sergeant Cutter hadn't decided to break tradition and come into work on the weekend. I'd put him in his place over the whole arresting Kevin thing and I he wasn't likely to forget it anytime soon. As it was, he had Kevin working every Saturday and Sunday and a few night shifts besides, just because my son had solved that whole poisoning case and made Cutter look like the kangaroo's backside that he is.

So when I hit the little customer bell at the counter I wasn't surprised to see Kevin come to the window. "Mom, I don't have anything new yet. You have to be a bit patient, right?"

"Sure, sure," I said, taking out one of the candy bars and opening it with more attention than it really deserved, trying to hide a smile. "I could be patient, or we could try to find Torey Walters."

"Well, that's the plan, Mom. Just don't know where to look. My source tracked her here for me but her trail just turns bottom up. I don't even know where to begin."

"I do."

The look of surprise on his face was pretty gratifying. I'd savor it more if I didn't feel like time was working against us. I can't really explain it. That's just the way it felt. Like there was some big grandfather clock in my head counting down the hours, minutes, seconds…

After I'd explained what Pastor Albright had said, Kevin just shook his head. "You got all that with just one visit to church?"

"Well. You know. The Lord works in mysterious ways and all that."

"So do you, apparently. Better come in and we'll make some phone calls. Seems like we're closer to the truth than we knew."

Closer? I really didn't feel like we were closer to the truth. It felt more like one step forward and two steps back to me.

Inside the station Kevin sat me down at a desk in the back interview room. We went through the information we had again, all our theories, and he had me repeat the description of Torey twice.

Finally, he nodded. "Yeah. That's her. I remember that tattoo."

Under his notepad was a folder. It was marked with Jess's name and as he opened it, I got a real sense of how much work he'd put into investigating her death so far. It was full of papers, printouts, and other pages. Leafing through it, Kevin made sure I didn't see anything a civilian wasn't supposed to, then brought out one form that had a bunch of typed information on it and a photo in the corner. It was black and white, but it perfectly fit the image of Torey Walters that I'd formed in my head.

"This is from our investigation of Roy Fittimer, drug dealer and all around waste of space." He tapped the photo thoughtfully. "So, I guess it's time to put out some missing posters and a BOLO message to the area police departments."

"Couldn't she still be in town?" I wondered out loud.

"It's a small town."

"Sure it is. But there's a lot of forest around to hide in. There's the quarry. Tons of hiking trails, too. I send tourists out to the trails all the time."

"You think our junky prostitute's been hiding out in the wilderness?" He arched an eyebrow at me, all smug like.

"You're assuming she's still alive."

"That's true. Could always be dead." He sighed, rubbing his hand through his hair. Obviously he hadn't considered that possibility. My Kevin is smart, but sometimes sons need to be reminded to listen to their mothers. "All right. Better call the other guys in. Get some volunteers to form search parties. The fire department guys train for this sort of thing out in the bush. Heh. Cutter's not gonna like this."

I bit my tongue rather than say how much I didn't care what Cutter liked. If we could find Torey, alive or not, then we might actually be closer to the truth. For real.

"Excuse me, Kevin?" Another officer opened the door after a single knock. Blake Williams, leaning in with a confused look on his face. "We letting the prisoner have his meds?"

Kevin sat up straighter. "Medicine? What medicine?"

"Brought them in from his room at the Inn. Hey, Miss Powers." He nodded to me, then hesitated to say anything more.

"Oh, strike a light, Blake." Kevin almost laughed at the other man. "It's not like she doesn't already know what's going on. This is Lakeshore, not Melbourne. It's not even Hobart, for that matter. We're all just folks here."

"Right. Right," Blake said, shrugging his shoulders. "No secrets in a small town. Not that this is a secret, I suppose. He just needs his medicines."

"What are they for?"

Blake looked back at him, blinking.

Kevin leaned back in his chair with a long breath as he crossed his heavy arms. "You didn't ask. Did you?"

With an annoyed scowl spreading over his face, Blake shook his head no.

"Well, maybe you should go ask him now," Kevin suggested, "before we give him something prescribed by a doctor. It, uh, is a prescription, right?"

"Of course it is. I'm not daft."

When Blake left the room Kevin looked at me with a meaningful glance. "Cutter's right hand man, you know."

"Heh. You should be the one in charge here, Kevin." This wasn't just a mother's pride talking. I know the score, and it isn't just me. "Everyone in town says the same thing."

Kevin rolled one shoulder. "I'm not the Senior Sergeant. I don't need to be. I just want to see the good folks of Lakeshore kept safe."

The way he said it might have sounded hokey coming from someone else. From him it was sincere. This was why he'd become a police officer in the first place.

"Well, someday I hope you have your shot at the top spot here," I tell him.

"Probably won't happen. It takes time to be promoted to Senior Sergeant. They won't just give the post to a constable. Won't be me."

I know he's right, but that doesn't mean I can't hope.

Blake comes back with a knock on the door. "Says it's for diabetes."

Kevin sat forward. "It's insulin?"

"No, uh," he lifted the medicine bottle in his hand to read the label, "Cycloset. Says to take every four hours. Been here a lot longer'n that. I think Cutter would want him to have his meds, right? Kevin?"

Without answering Kevin stood up from the desk and took the pill bottle from Blake, then he was off down the hallway.

We followed him right to the holding cells at the back. There's just the two of them, side by side between two cinder block walls. The front wall is these thick iron bars spaced closely enough that the people inside couldn't squeeze through. The wall between the cells was more bars.

In the cell on the right, Horace sat with his arms and legs crossed and a scowl on his face. When he saw the bottle in Kevin's hand he jumped up from the little bench and stuck his hand through the bars. "About time. I need that, ya know."

"So I'm told," Kevin said to him, standing just out of his reach with the bottle. "Tell me why you need this."

"Already told your other guy. I'm a diabetic. Type two diabetes. Easy to maintain, if I get my bloody medicine!" He glared daggers at all three of us. "Have to stay away from sweets and exercise on a regular basis, too, and oh yeah it helps if I don't get too stressed out. Like by being arrested for something I didn't do!"

My eyebrows shot up. That's why Kevin had been so interested in what Horace's medicine was for. Horace had to stay away from sweets. Diabetic medication and no sweets.

All those little hard candy wrappers in the dust bin. Where they'd found the key. The killer had been sucking on candy while he waited to…do that to Jess.

The killer had a sweet tooth, and Horace couldn't have sweets. Certainly not that many at a time.

Kevin caught my eye as he handed the bottle over to Blake and instructed him to give Horace the dosage. For a moment I felt like the world had just been yanked out from under my feet. I had to turn away, walk away, hold my head down so my son wouldn't see me cry.

Horace wasn't the killer. He couldn't be.

You don't know him, Jess had been trying to tell me. I should have listened.

I didn't know her killer.

I might not understand Horace, but I knew this devil.

Out there, somewhere, was a devil I didn't know.

CHAPTER TEN

Back at the Inn I made sure that one of my employees had the desk covered. We weren't scheduled to have any arrivals come in for the next two days, but that didn't mean we wouldn't have a tourist wander into town at some odd hour and need a room.

Here's to hoping it turned out better for them than it had for Jess.

I went straight up to my room. As I walked down the second floor hallway there was this pressure that made my skin tingle. It broke over me as I went past room seven, unseen and ephemeral, like walking through spider webs. I didn't even stop outside of Jess's room. Couldn't bring myself to do it this time.

My own room had never felt so big and empty to me. Not since before Richard had left. My hubby. It hadn't been easy, getting past that kind of betrayal. It almost would have been better if he'd died. At least then there would have been closure. All he'd left me with was questions without answers.

I was hungry, and I was bone tired, and I was so frustrated I couldn't even cry. Someone had snuck into the Inn—*my* Inn—and then killed my friend and now it looked like they were going to get away with it.

So. I could go down to lunch and let Rosie make me something to eat. I could crawl into bed and sleep the rest of this whole day away. I could even curl up into a tight little ball and just wait for tomorrow to come.

Choices, choices.

Another option occurred to me. A warm soak in the tub. Just what every girl needs, sometimes. I'd like a glass of beer to go with it, or two, but that would mean I'd have to go downstairs again. I'd rather just hide in my room for a while, I think.

Seashells greet me as I open the connecting door to the bathroom. Maybe it was time to change the décor in here. It was a sight too cheerful for my state of mind. Stripping out of my shirt and my pants, kicking them over in the corner, I push aside the semi-transparent shower curtain around the tub about to turn on the hot water.

"Heya, Dell."

I was too scared to scream even though I needed to. It welled up into my throat and choked me and made my blood cold. Throwing myself backward I slipped and fell, going down hard, my head bouncing against the floor. A ringing rose up in my ears. Pain brought me back to my senses.

Jess had been standing in the shower. She was gone now, the room empty again except for me, but I know what I saw. It had been Jess, with that crooked smile of hers and those eyes full of mischief. She'd been wearing the same ripped jeans and form fitting t-shirt. The Jess that I remembered being so alive and vibrant.

Gone now.

Using the bathroom sink for leverage I made it to my feet again. There was a lump at the back of my head that throbbed in time to my pulse. I could feel it rising under my gently probing fingers, under my hair. Was I bleeding? That had been a pretty hard knock.

"Jess," I said to the air around me, "don't do things like that."

In the medicine cabinet mirror I tried to see the damage.

Except I couldn't, because it was fogged over. I hadn't even run the bathwater yet, and it was fogged over.

In the misty condensation of the glass a single word was written. *Mine*.

⁓

A bite to eat suddenly sounded right good to me.

If it was an excuse to get me out of my bathroom, out of my room, I didn't care and I didn't argue the point. Believing in ghosts is one thing. Having them leave cryptic, possessive messages on my bathroom mirror is something else entirely.

Whatever Jess was claiming as hers—*mine*—I was very certain I didn't want to have any part of it.

It never occurred to me that any other ghostly hand could have written that message. It's not like my Inn has a whole bunch of ghosts running around to choose from.

I rushed into the dining room just about fifteen minutes later. Time enough to wipe the message away and see it reform itself, throw my clothes back on, and lock the door behind me.

Don't ask me why I did that last step. From everything I know, ghosts can walk right through a locked door. I suppose it just made me feel better.

Through the dining room and into the kitchen behind, I was watched by a singular set of eyes. I'd missed the lunch rush, and the place was empty except for Mister Brewster. His odd-colored eyes followed me, his elbows folded on the table and his interlaced fists resting against his chin. He regarded me with a serious look. Like he was examining me.

I noticed there was a glass of water in front of him along with an untouched turkey club sandwich. I've never seen the man eat.

He orders his food, and then he sits with it, and after a while it just seems to disappear bit by bit.

He pays for his room a month in advance, I told myself. As long as his money was good he could be as creepy as he wanted to be.

I wonder if he's ever seen a ghost?

The thought was so sudden that it stopped me at the swinging door to the kitchen. I'd never consider asking that question of one of the other guests for fear that they'd pack up their things and leave the Inn, the state, maybe even the country itself. But Mister Brewster was, well, creepy enough that maybe he wouldn't spook at the thought of having a recently deceased neighbor living in the next room over.

Then again…

He pays his rent in advance, I reminded myself.

Pushing through the door I left Mister Brewster to his meal.

Rosie was directing the washing and tidying up of the lunch dishes. She's a very hands-on kind of boss, and the employees who work the kitchen or the dining room know that about her and respect her for it. As I watched, she waved a white towel at one of them, shooing them to go faster, then tossed the cloth aside.

It landed on the griddle, still slick with hot grease, and in two seconds flat we had a small fire blossoming right there in our kitchen.

Fortunately that's such a common occurrence that the staff doesn't even blink over it anymore. Without missing a beat on his way to the sink with an armful of dirty plates, Paul picked up the container of white flour and poured it liberally over the stove top. Still walking, he passed me with a wink.

"I'll clean that up in a sec, Miss Powers."

"Thanks Paul," I whisper back.

When Rosie turns around again to see her stove covered in flour, she throws her hands in the air. "What is this? I can't turn my back on you lot for a minute. Paul, clean this up straight away!"

"Will do, Rosie." With another wink at me, he sets his plates in the sink to be washed and attends to the near disaster.

"Lord above, Dell," Rosie says to me. "We've got to get ready for dinner service and it's still chaos in here. What'ya been up to? Haven't seen you all day."

"Um. Well, that's kind of a long story." I'm going to tell her all of it, and I know that. I think that's why I really came down here in the first place. "Mind if I make a sandwich first so I can talk and eat at the same time?"

"Oh, no need. Gretchen, can you get Dell some of that three-cheese macaroni, please? Wait till ya try this, Dell. Make your taste-buds dance, it will!"

I never doubt my friend's culinary opinion. When the dish is set down on the center island in front of me, the smell makes my mouth water. But, I stand there, looking straight at Rosie with a patient little smile on my face.

"Oh, my," she says, immediately seeing what I need. "Everyone out, please. Take a half hour break and be back ready to go. Yes. Scoot, please. Thanks. Good job, everyone! Best lunch service in a long time. I mean it!"

When the kitchen is clear of everyone but us, I take a breath, choke back a few frustrated tears, and tell her everything that's happened in this one, impossibly short day.

Rosie's eyes were comically big before I ran out of things to say. Not that any of this was funny.

"I can't believe it," she said. "I thought all of this was behind us. Horace isn't the one who did it? Then who is? I can't believe this."

"Me either." The only part I left out of my story was what had just happened to me up in the bathroom. Considering Pastor Albright's reaction I can only imagine what Rosie's would be. "This mac and cheese is wonderful, by the way. I haven't had time to eat all day. Well, except for some candy bars."

"Well I can imagine. I'm so sorry, Dell. I, um, may have been unkind before in the things I said about Jess."

"You were being truthful, Rosie. That's all." I put another few bites of my lunch away. Or was it dinner? I've lost all track. "So, I guess the rest of it is up to Kevin and them. Him and the volunteers and the rest of the force are going to look around the town. We need to find this Torey woman. I sure don't know where to look."

Pulling a stool over to sit across from me at the island counter, Rosie took up a fork and stole some of my mac and cheese. "Well, sure," she said around a mouthful of food. "That makes sense."

Her eyes stay focused on the food when she says it, and from the way she chose her words so carefully it was like she was doing her best to keep from saying Torey might already be dead.

Which was the same thought I've had in the back of my head all along. I just can't let it be true. She needs to be out there, somewhere. She might be the only one who knows who really did this to Jess.

"There are lots of places to hide out there," I remind Rosie.

"Right," she agreed, a little too enthusiastically. "I mean, there's the woods, and um, more woods, and the trails of course, and the quarry."

"That's exactly what I told my Kevin…" With a sharp gasp, choking on a bite of food, I realize what we just said. I sit there, staring at Rosie, coughing, as it finally clicks in my head.

Why hadn't I seen it before?

"Rosie, I have to go." I take another huge bite of the mac and cheese, because it really is amazing and I really am hungry, but I have to go see Kevin. I need to let him know.

"Dell? Are you all right?" she asks me.

Now there's a loaded question.

"Can you watch the Inn for me for a little bit longer? I don't know how long I'll be."

She picked up my plate and put it in front of her, intent on finishing it off. "Can do. I hope you find what you're looking for."

"Me too." I can't tell her all of it yet. If I'm right, then maybe I understand what Jess wrote in my mirror.

I hold my unicorn necklace tight as I rush outside.

The sun is heading down toward the horizon when I step out of the Inn. I don't own a car. Kevin has one that I borrow whenever I need to drive out to Hobart or anywhere else outside of Lakeshore. There's the rental the Inn has, too, but I don't have a car of my own.

What I do have, is a bicycle.

The Wallaby is the little red ten speed that I've had with me since University. I named her myself. She could use a coat of paint, and I never quite get around to greasing the chain like I mean to, but she makes getting from one end of the town to the other a lot easier when I'm in a hurry.

The wind whips through my long hair now as I cycle through the gears and bring myself to the police station in a fraction of the time it would have taken me to walk. There are a lot of cars here. I recognize some of them. Police officers, firemen, others from the town. Near the back of the line is a beat up green Volkswagon Beetle, the old kind that actually had the engine in the back. I recognize that one, too.

James Callahan stood outside his car, scribbling in his notebook, making sure to take note of everyone who came and went. I guess that means I'll be in his next edition of the Lakeshore Times, too.

He smiles at me as I step down from the Wallaby and walk my bicycle up the line of cars. "Hey, Dell. How's things?"

"You tell me, James. I'm just here to see my son." I feel bad for lying to him, because I had promised to fill him in on what was happening in the investigation, but this part of it has to stay secret. For now.

With a smile and a shake of his head he shoved his pencil into the spiral wiring of his notebook. "I was hoping ya could trust me more'n that, Dell."

"I do trust you, James." I was surprised to hear myself say that. We were friends, sure, but I didn't know him all that well. Just from around town. That, and the long talk we'd had at the Milkbar. "I, uh, need to see Kevin. Can I call you later to tell you what I've found out?"

His smile is warm. "I'd like that."

I turn away with my face heating, and hook my hair back behind my ear like a schoolgirl. There's a mix of emotions inside of me and I don't know what to do about them. Except ignore them. For now. James is a nice guy, a handsome man, and maybe if my good friend hadn't just died I would have taken some time to talk to him.

He was cute. Amazing how I'd never noticed that before.

I had to push through knots of people talking and standing around to get into the police station. I'm pretty much ignored as I go in. Everyone is keyed up, ready to go on this hunt. Something like this doesn't happen here. The last time was when Eliza Batiste's daughter went missing and the fire department went on a three hour search of the woods only to finally find the six year old asleep in her own closet.

They were ready for some real excitement this time.

I found Kevin in Senior Sergeant Cutter's office, along with Blake and the fire chief. Kevin was surprised to see me, but it was Cutter's reaction that filled the room.

"What d'ya think you're doing in here?" he bellowed, and every eye in the room turned to stare at me.

"Uh, I needed Kevin for a minute."

"I don't give a brass razoo! This is a police station, Miss Powers! Ya don't just waltz in here to have a convo with yer little boy!"

I really hate this man. "Listen, Cutter, I ought to give you—"

"Senior Sergeant I'll take her out," Kevin said in a quick staccato, making sure to grab me by my elbow before I could say another word. He steered me through everyone to the back of the station.

I couldn't help but notice that Horace was gone already when we went by the holding cells.

Instead of walking me out the back door Kevin stopped by an empty stretch of hallway where a corkboard held notices about criminal activity and a full color map of the town and the area around us.

"Kevin, what are you doing!" I blurt out. "I was just about to give Cutter a piece of my mind."

"D'ya think that might be why I did it?" He smiled at me even though I could see the stress he was under. "He's on my case on this one, Mom. Again, I might add. It's not gonna look good for me if my mom comes popping in to tuck my nappie into my shirt."

He took a breath, then shook his head at himself. "Sorry. Sorry, you didn't deserve that. That was Cutter talking, not me."

I figured as much, but it still stung. Cutter wasn't the one standing here mouthing the words.

"What was it you needed?" he asks me, in a kinder voice.

I hadn't been able to think up a good way to explain this to him. So, I'd settled on the direct approach. "I know where Torey is."

"What? How?"

"Call it...a mother's intuition." That would have to do for now because I wasn't about to go into more detail. Reaching past him to point at the map on the wall, I stick my finger at the exact spot he'll need to direct the search. "Right here."

Kevin turned, and leaned in to squint at the spot. "That's the rock quarry. It's not open for the season yet."

"Exactly. All of those tunnels into the rocks, plus the supply sheds with canned rations for the workers. It's the perfect spot to hide out. Torey could stay there for a couple of weeks, before the crews come in to start digging again."

He thought about it, one hand rubbing at his chin. "The rock quarry. With the tunnels where they mine dolerite."

"Exactly," I agree.

The quarry. Also known as…

The mine.

CHAPTER ELEVEN

Time moves on. That's a favorite saying of mine.

Then there's days where time stands perfectly still and goes absolutely nowhere.

The ride back to the Inn was one of the longest in my life. In reality, of course, it didn't take me any more time than it ever did. It just felt like I was forever and a day getting back.

What would happen when we found Torey? What could she tell us about Jess's killer? What if I was wrong about the message in the mirror, for that matter? Hey, for all I knew Jess was saying she really liked that mirror and wanted to claim it as her own.

No. I don't think that's how it works, either.

Thing is, I'm not as practiced at this whole ghost business as Darcy Sweet is. It's all new to me. Like, I still can't believe it. That kind of new. So, maybe I don't know all the sorts of ghostly things that ghosts do, but I'm willing to bet they don't waste energy scribbling out a furniture wish list. Jess had been telling me where to find Torey. In the mine.

Kevin was already in hot water for having his mommy show up at the station during such an important operation. It wasn't like I was going to be invited to join the volunteers on the search. So, off I went, gone home to wait for word that they've found Torey.

Alive, I have to add. That they find her alive.

The searchers wouldn't be able to be out for very long before they'd have to call it a night. Sunset was upon us as I reached the Inn, at the end of the big hill on Fenlong Street. From here, the view of Pine Lake is spectacular. The way the dying colors of the sun paint the tips of the gentle waves red and orange. The way the water laps at the shoreline. The dark, scraggly Monteray pines that stand silent watch over the water.

A pair of grebes swooped out over the middle of the lake, splashing down with a rustling of wings, looking for a dinner of bugs and fish. It's a beautiful place, Lakeshore is.

It's getting a little darker than it used to be. And I'm not talking about the sunset.

I stow the Wallaby away into the Inn's storage shed along with the holiday decorations and boxes of cleaning supplies and lightbulbs and other oddments. Don't know when I'll need it next but it's good to know it'll be there for me when I do.

Inside the Inn, I notice two things right away, each one just as surprising as the other.

First, George somehow managed to hang the portrait of the honored Lieutenant Governor up on that spot on the wall.

Second, there's a man sitting in one of our chairs from the common room, pulled out here into the foyer. He's leaning back in it with the top resting against the wall and two legs off the floor, right under old David Collins's face.

Where am I supposed to begin with something like that?

He smiled at me and gestures with the bowler hat in his hand. "Sorry, love. Wasn't sure when you was gonna be back, so I made meself to home."

His accent is more British than Australian, although an untrained ear probably wouldn't notice the difference. Americans, for instance, usually say we all sound alike. He was sort of tall but very thin, sitting there in my chair like an upstart child in school. His dark hair was cut short and then shaved on the sides. His face was all sharp angles and stubbly beard growth. Like a GQ model who was moonlighting as a grim reaper.

Okay, maybe that's a little dramatic but even his suit fits the part. Gray, with white pinstripes, and a blue silk tie. His watch was probably the real article and not a knockoff which meant it was worth more'n most Taswegians earned in a year.

"Uh, can I help you?" I asked him. I noticed there was no one at the front desk. It wasn't like Rosie to leave that unattended when there was a guest out here or in the commons room. There wasn't much cash behind the counter but there was enough that we didn't want some light-fingered bugaboo slipping back there.

"Don't worry none about your business partner," the man said to me, settling his chair down on all four legs with a hard thump. "Sent her back to the kitchen with a special request. She does love to cook, now don't she?"

Above him, the portrait of David Collins shook, but stayed where it was. What had George done, glued the thing to the wall? "Sir, I wouldn't sit—"

"Antonio, Miss Powers. The name's Antonio Ferarro. Under normal circumstances, I'm sure I'd be pleased to make your acquaintance."

There was a cold vibe coming off him that settled across me in waves. I went around to the space behind the counter where at least I would have that little bit of furniture between me and him. I felt like I needed a barrier between us. Plus easy access to the phone, which had the police department's number and Kevin's on speed dial.

'Course, that wouldn't do me much good when they were all in the bush around town looking for a missing witness.

Oh, snap.

I cleared my throat, realizing the only thing I can do is keep him talking. "Was there something you needed me to do for you, Mister Ferarro?"

He leaned forward to put his elbows on his knees and spin the curved brim of his bowler hat between the tips of his fingers. "Well, like I says, these are not normal circumstances. I'm here on what you might call business. It's a right nasty business, too." The hat stopped spinning. "It would seem that you are about to find the elusive Torey Walters for us. I've been looking for her meself, to be sure, but I didn't have a Danny where she'd be. She's a right slippery…uh, crafty lady. Tell the truth I was getting tired of tramping through those pine trees of yours anyway. Got me knickers in a right twist, it did."

I'm sure my mouth was open. He smiled at me in a "gotchya" kind of way and I had to remind myself that this man wasn't here on a social call. Freezing up in front of him, like a deer in headlights, was probably not my best course. "How do you know about Torey Walters?"

"Well, that there's the big question." He set that hat square on his head and leaned the chair back against the wall once more. Thump. "See, Torey has something that belongs to us. She's…an associate of ours, you might parlay. Sure. An associate. Thing is, she took something of ours, and we needs it back."

"That doesn't explain why you're here. In my Inn."

He cleared his throat, and started tapping the back of the chair against the wall. Thump, thump, thump. "Seems she was supposed to be coming to stay here. Leastwise, that's the tale the pastor spins. Bit dodgy, that bloke. Like he sees spooks in every corner."

"You spoke to Pastor Albright?" My hand kept hovering over toward the phone. Calling for help seemed like the best idea I'd had all day.

"Too right. The good pastor and I had a long chat. Well, a short one, but still. We knew she'd be coming here anyways. Not like there's a lot of places to stay in Lakeshore, now is there?"

"I don't know how I can help you, Mister Ferarro."

"Seriously," he said over me, "it's a bitty flyspeck of a place, now ain't it?"

All the while, he thumped his chair back against the wall. Thump. Thump.

Thump.

"Maybe I should just call my son," I suggested, with emphasis. "He's a policeman."

"No need for that," he said, his smile stiff. "He's off chasing our Miss Torey, now ain't he? Let's have him do his job while you and I go have us a chat, somewhere private, so's I can explain what happens to folks that don't do what we ask. See, Torey stashed some poppy what don't belong to her. Got herself in a spot of trouble. Don't want that to happen to you."

His accent makes it hard to follow, but I get the gist of it. Torey stole from this man's "associates." He wants to get back whatever it is she took.

No honor among thieves, after all.

From the way he's sitting, I can see the bottoms of his shoes. I really wish he wouldn't do that, bang the chair against the wall like that, and I'm about to tell him so when I notice the tread on his shoes is oddly familiar.

"So, shall we walk outside for a bit?"

"I don't think so," I answer, slowly taking the receiver off the hook, and feeling the speed dial numbers with my fingertips. "I think I'd rather stay right here."

"Oh, but I insist."

His hand goes into the inside of his suitcoat.

My heart leaps up and I press the buttons for the first preset in the speed dial.

At the same time, he thumps the chair back down to the floor. *Thump.*

From an inside pocket, he takes out a brightly colored candy wrapper.

Just as Rosie comes back in from the kitchen.

"Who's ready for some raspberry tart?"

And the painting falls off the wall with a jerky leap and lands edge-first on top of Mister Antonio Ferarro's bowler hat.

It probably looked funnier than it was.

No. No, it was pretty funny. Well. I did tell him not to sit like that.

"Rosie come with me," I tell her without waiting to see if Ferraro survived his run-in with Tasmania's first lieutenant governor. I grab her by the hand and drag her up the stairs and straight to Jess's room. I have it locked but the master key is in my pocket and we dodge inside before I close the door tight and lock it again.

Why did I choose here? That's a good question. I'm not really sure. I know there are a few other empty rooms on this floor. The one next door where Horace had been staying, for instance. But I came here without even hesitating. I didn't even go up to my room.

The stains from Jess's death are still visible on the floor and the rest of the room is in the same state of disarray that Kevin and I had left it. I still can't do anything with it. Not until the investigation is over.

Which it isn't.

Yet.

Rosie is staring at me, her eyes probing mine, trying to read my thoughts. Trying to figure out why I'm playing this game of hide and seek. After a handful of heavy heartbeats she holds out the plate in her hands with her fresh baked tart on it. "Want some?" she asks.

In Rosie's world, food makes just about anything better. I've eaten her food. In most cases, she's right.

"Rosie, that man downstairs, did he say anything to you?"

She lifted the plate again, as if raspberry tart explains everything. "He asked me to make him some dessert."

"Okay, um, anything else?"

"No." She shook her head at me, then looked down at the pastry in her hand. "I just made him a tart."

In the hall I can hear footsteps. "Shh. Rosie, don't say anything."

Her eyes grow bigger, and she nods her head, probably not understanding a single thing that's going on but trusting my judgment just the same. The footsteps thud down the hallway, closer, and closer.

Then they stop. Right on the other side of this door.

Of course. I should have expected that. Of course he would know where this room is.

I work the cord on my unicorn necklace until the little wooden pendant is in my hand. Jess's last gift to me. A talisman left by a friend.

The handle rattles as Ferraro tries it from the outside. So glad I thought to lock it.

Very suddenly his footsteps turn away, back up the hall. Then they stop again.

Wait. Did I lock the room where Horace was staying?

Rosie and I stare at each other as we hear that door open, then hear the muted footsteps walk inside.

No. I didn't lock it.

Isn't that just bonza.

All this time, Ferraro hasn't said a word. He's silently acting out some plan, I just can't figure out what it is. Following him with my ears through the wall, imagining him moving across the floor in the room next door, I hear him at the window.

I hear the window latch rattling.

Oh.

Ferraro's going to open the window, and jump across to this room here. There's no doubt in my mind that he'll make the jump.

He did the same thing the night he killed Jess, after all.

The shoe print. The candies he had in his pocket. This was Jess's killer.

Next to me, Rosie closed her eyes, and I can hear her quietly praying. She still has the raspberry tart in her hands as she asks God to keep us safe.

I'm all for prayer, but I know that whole line about *faith without works being dead.* If we want to be safe, we should get out of here, now, as quiet as two church mice.

"Rosie," I whisper, before something steals my breath away.

Over at the window, transparent and as substantial as shadow, I see Jess. She flipped her hair back over her shoulder, and winked at me.

I can't say anything at all. I can only watch as she faded through the window, moving outside.

Now I know why I brought me and Rosie here. It was the one place in the Inn where I knew I'd feel safe from that man.

Because it was the one place that I knew I'd find Jess waiting for me.

That thought is only just in my head when I hear the scream from the other room, a man's cry of surprise, then a loud crash and the sounds of Ferraro scrambling across the room and out into the hallway. I can faintly hear him running down the stairs.

He's gone. I can imagine what happened. He saw…something. Maybe he didn't even know that it was Jess he saw. However it looked to him, it scared him enough that he slipped on the open windowsill and fell back into the room, and then he ran away with his tail between his legs.

I put my hand on Rosie's shoulder, shaking her out of her state. Her eyes popped open and she looked up at me. In a whisper, she asked, "Is he gone?"

"Yes. He, uh, couldn't stay. Something scared him off."

Crossing herself, she balanced the raspberry tart in one hand, looking down at it in surprise. "Well. I suppose he won't be wanting this, then."

I have to laugh. Leave it to Rosie to put the whole thing into perspective.

Together, we went downstairs again, slowly, careful to keep an eye out in case Ferraro is still here. He's not, but on my registration counter is a memento. His crushed bowler, with a note beside it, the pen from the guestbook laid neatly across the small piece of paper.

You ruined my hat. I'll be back to collect.

The phone rings at that exact moment, making me jump, the note dropping from my hand. Behind me, Rosie drops her tart. The plate smashes against the floor.

I grab the phone up and put it to my ear. It was off the receiver, from my failed attempt to call for help, but the secondary line is the one that's ringing. When I press the flashing button, I hear my son's voice.

"Mom? Mom," Kevin said, his voice filled with excitement. "We got her. Found her right there in the quarry just like you thought!"

My mind was racing. They had Torey Walters. I looked down at the bowler hat, one long vertical crease running its length, and remember Antonio Ferraro's promise to come back and collect his revenge. "Kevin, you can't bring Torey here."

"Whassat? How'd ya know I was gonna ask?"

"Because I know you. Listen, she can not come here. Okay? Put her…no, don't tell me where you're going to put her. Just find someplace safe for her and come over to the Inn straight after, all right?"

I look over at the portrait of David Collins, laying on the floor, once again knocked off that wall by a force I can only guess at. I wonder if he ever had to deal with things like this.

"Just get here as fast as you can, all right Kevin? We just found Jess's real killer."

⸺

"How did he know?"

That was the same question I'd been wondering at, along with a dozen or so other things. Like why Jess's murderer was still in town.

Well. That one sort of answered itself. Whatever group Antonio was working for, his business associates, wanted the money Torey had stolen from them. Wanted it badly enough to kill for it.

And they weren't going to leave until they had it back.

"I mean," Kevin was saying, sipping his coffee, "we only figured out she was in town, what, yesterday? They knew we were looking for her before we even got started. How?"

"They could've been staking out the police station," Rosie offered.

The three of us were sitting at a table in the dining room. Now that it was after dark the Inn was quiet. A few of the guests sat out in the common room watching television together but where we were, the three of us were alone. We'd been talking about this for an hour or better now, and Rosie's suggestion was the best we'd come up with. How did Antonio know Kevin and the others were going to go looking for Torey?

"Maybe this man was watching us," Kevin agreed. "This Antonio Ferarro. The alternative is that someone ratted on us to him. I'd hate to think any of our officers were in bed with whoever this man is."

His hand fists around the coffee mug. He had been mad enough to know that some bloke had been in here threatening me. Now he had to imagine one of his own people was the reason it had happened. I could see the rage in his eyes.

That's my Kevin. Still looking out for his mom.

"Did Torey tell you anything?" I asked him.

"She's being pretty tight-lipped. Scared, is what she is. Cutter's interviewing her. You can imagine how that's going."

Rosie and I share a look. Cutter. The shining example of law enforcement in Lakeshore.

"We did find her mobile on her." That brought a sour smile to Kevin's face. "It'd been shut off for a while, but lots of missed calls from a single number. When we tried to ring it back the call went straight to voicemail. The message says Antonio can't take a call right now."

I turn my cup around on the table. Antonio. He'd been trying to find Torey for days. Ever since he found out that he'd killed the wrong girl. "So, we're thinking that he killed Jess by mistake?"

"No. Not by mistake. He was here for Torey, sure, and he expected to find her here. But he sedated your friend. He probably asked her all his questions first, wanting to know what she knew. Then he…"

He stopped talking, and I'm grateful for that, but I've got the image in my head already. Antonio sat Jess in that chair, drugged up, and after finding out she didn't know where to find Torey either, he slit her wrists and left her for us to find. It should've looked like a suicide. Did look like one to Cutter. Too bad for Antonio we figured it out.

Too bad for Jess we weren't just that much smarter. We might have saved her life.

Tears made me blink my eyes over and over until I could see clearly again. Now we knew for sure who killed Jess. We just had to find him and make him stand trial. My friend deserved that kind of justice.

Which reminded me. "Where's Horace gone off to?"

Kevin chuckled. "He left town. Said he'd had enough of us dills here in the backside of Woop Woop."

When Rosie and I both stare at him, he added, "His words. Not mine."

Rosie shifted in her seat. "Well. That was rude."

"That's the Horace we remember, now isn't it?" I shrug my shoulders. "Then again, we did arrest him for killing his wife when he really didn't."

"Don't make him a nice man, now does it?" Rosie asks.

Across the room, in the reflection of a window where night is pressing in from outside, I thought for just a moment that I could see Jess. She was laughing at our comments. Horace. A real git. That made her laugh.

Then the image was gone, and I was sure I imagined it.

Only, I didn't imagine it up in the room when Jess saved us from Antonio. And I didn't imagine that word left on my mirror. And I didn't imagine the dream with Jess that led me to the first real clues in this whole crazy mystery.

So did I really imagine it now?

Either way, when I look for her again she's gone.

"Any idea how they knew which room Jess would be in?" Rosie asked while pouring more cream in her coffee. "I mean, there's two floors up there and sixteen rooms. How'd they know which one?"

"We found text messages from Jess on Torey's phone." Kevin pushed his cup away. "She told Torey to meet her here in room seven. Right after that's when the phone got shut off. Guess she saw the police vehicles here when Jess died. Not sure how Antonio knew what room Jess was in though. Maybe Torey told him or he heard about it around town. Something like that. So that's means, motive, opportunity. All the right elements to solve a crime except one."

"Which one?" I asked him.

"The most important one. Where our suspect is."

"Well, we know where he's going to be," I pointed out. "He's going to come back here."

"Are ya sure?" Rosie asked. The idea obviously didn't set well with her. "He has to know the police are looking for him now, right?"

"I agree," Kevin said. "He tried to scare you into helping him, Mom, and you and Rosie beat him off. Not likely he'll be back anytime soon."

Not that me and Rosie had anything to do with Antonio being scared off. Still. "I don't think this guy is going to give up that easily. He'll be back."

"What makes you think that?"

"Isn't it obvious? I ruined his hat."

For a moment Kevin just stared at me, before he burst out laughing.

CHAPTER TWELVE

Somehow, Kevin convinced me to come stay with him for the night. I can't remember the last night I spent away from the Inn.

His place isn't big. Just a shoebox on one of Lakeshore's sidestreets. One bedroom, one bathroom, one small living room off the kitchen and dining room area. It's always been just enough for him. Now, it was enough for him and his houseguest.

Ellie Burlick fit nicely into this space, I thought. I can't believe my son has kept their relationship such a secret all these months. From me.

So much for a mother's intuition.

Which put me on the couch tonight while he and Ellie slept in his bed. I feel kind of bad, actually, because it's her last night here in Tasmania. Tomorrow she's back to the mainland. Got a job that won't let her stay away for too long.

Although, I heard them talking when they thought I was already asleep. Seems she might be able to transfer to Hobart. Also seems she's seriously considering it.

I've been through a lot of pain in the last few days. Knowing Kevin has found love in his life goes a long way to making me feel better. Life goes on, after all.

I fought sleep for a long time, because I'm so very sure that Antonio Ferraro is going to come through a window and sit there across from me popping little candies into his mouth, and tell me he owes me for ruining his hat.

When that doesn't happen, I finally let myself drift until I can't remember if I'm awake or not.

"Hi."

I don't think I was even dreaming yet. When someone sat down in the chair down by the end of the couch, and spoke that one word, I sat bolt upright. At first, I was sure it was going to be Jess. At this point it wouldn't surprise me if she walked through the front door and asked me out to lunch for a long talk about how nice Heaven is.

It's not her. It's Ellie.

She's wrapped in a blue flannel robe. If I remember correctly blue is her favorite color. Can't help but notice this robe's one of my son's. In the dim light of the reading lamp on the end table her dark blonde hair is the color of gold spilling loosely around her neck. Usually she has her hair in a perfect tail, but here she's at her ease. The way she's sitting, with one leg up on the glass coffee table, makes the shoulders of the too-big robe slip down her arms. She's wearing a purple pajama top underneath. Straight from bed, then.

'Course, there's only the one bedroom, and my son's home too, so that paints the picture just about as vividly as a mother needs to see it.

"What time is it?" I ask blearily. Rubbing my eyes, I look around for a clock. Kevin's apartment is such a bachelor pad.

"It's still late," Ellie said to me. "Or, early I guess. Depends on which side of midnight you're standing on. Sorry to wake you. I, um, wanted to talk. Um. About your son."

"You two are spending a lot of time together, he tells me."

"Yeah. We were trying to keep it a secret. Not from you. Please understand, Dell. I didn't want ya thinking we were ashamed of what we're doing."

"Ellie, I understand. Really. The whole thing with your sister… it complicates things."

She sighed out a heavy breath, grateful for my words. I can begin to see now how hard it's been on her. "You know my friend was killed here, right? I'm sure Kevin told you. I can understand how hard it's been for you since your sister died. I'm glad you have someone like my Kevin to keep you company and make life better."

"He really does," she admitted with a little quirk of a smile. "Your Kevin is one of the special ones, Dell."

"Thank you. I like to take most of the credit for that, seeing as how his father saw fit to leave us a few years back."

Ellie was silent for a moment, playing with her fingertips, tracing the lines of her beautifully manicured nails. "Didn't mean to bring up bad memories," she said to me. "Just wanted to make sure me and you are all right. Sometimes a mother can be very protective of her son."

"Oh, I am. But Kevin has grown up to be able to take care of himself. He's a good man now, and I can tell he's picked a good one with you."

"I lucked out with him, that's the truth. Well. I should let you get back to sleep. He told me what happened over at your Inn. That's just awful. Any idea how this Antonio bloke knew the police were homing in on Torey?"

All I can do is shake my head. That's the only big question left in all of this. That, and where Antonio has disappeared to. Lakeshore isn't that big a town, and everyone knows everyone else, and unless he's learned to sleep in trees like a koala, he has to be…somewhere.

"I don't know how he found out," I said to her. "I know he came after me because Jess was my friend and he thought maybe she told me something. Plus, Kevin's my son. Maybe he thought I had some kind of inside information."

Inside information…

"Dell, are you all right?"

Ellie's question is a faint sound over the buzzing in my ears. My thoughts spin me back to yesterday, at the police station, when all of the officers and firemen and volunteers were getting ready to go hunt for Torey, not knowing if she'd be alive or dead. When Cutter had all but thrown me out because I wasn't supposed to be there.

"I have to go."

Throwing my blanket off, surprising Ellie, I get up off the couch and start fumbling in my overnight bag for a change of clothes.

"Dell," she said to me, "you can't leave yet."

"I know it's early, but I have to go check into something." Then I stop. It is insanely early. Nobody will be up at this hour. Well, the man I'm going to see might be. And if he is, we're going to have a very long conversation. If he's not up, I'll wake him up. "I have to go."

"You can't leave yet."

Her voice is strange. Different than it was a few seconds ago.

"I have to," I repeated, hoping that's the end of it.

"You can't leave yet."

"Why not?"

"Dell," she insists, "look at me."

Turning to her, clothes spilling over in my arms, I see that it isn't Ellie in the chair anymore.

Sitting there now, in that loose fitting blue robe, is Jess.

I dropped my things to the floor, standing frozen in place, watching the ghost of my friend as she points to the front door. "If you leave now," she said to me, "he'll get you."

The front door bursts inward in a shower of splinters and a screech of metal. Antonio Ferarro follows, walking inside as calm as can be, that cold smile curling his mouth into a sneer.

"You ruined my hat," he said to me, just before he raises his huge black gun, takes aim at me, and pulls the trigger.

With a gasp of air that nearly chokes me I sit bolt upright on the couch, shaking and feeling across my chest and torso for a bullet wound that wasn't there. A dream. Just a dream. A very bad, very vivid dream. Laying back down on the couch my arm fell over the side and down to the floor, where it brushes against something.

I look down to see the clothes that I had taken out of my bag, in my dream, and then dropped right where they are now.

"Hi."

Ellie Burlick plops herself into the chair at the end of the couch, wearing my son's blue robe, her dark blonde hair spilling over her slender shoulders. "Sorry to wake you. I, um, wanted to talk. Um. About your son."

I sit up again. It's all happening. The same exact way it just did in my dream. Ellie coming out to talk to me about Kevin, wearing his robe, nervous of what I think about the two of them dating. All of it, happening all over again.

Which means…

"Kevin!" I yelled, jumping up off the couch, throwing the blanket aside, surprising Ellie. "Kevin get up! He's here. He's outside the house!"

"Dell, what are you—" Ellie never finished her sentence. The sound of glass breaking makes us both drop down, and I feel more than see the bullet zip by me to hit the wall two feet in front of me. The thunder of the gunshot follows immediately.

Then silence falls all around us.

"Mom?" I hear my son calling out. He's moving in the bedroom and I can imagine him hastily yanking on a pair of pants as he takes his .45 automatic from the drawer where he keeps it. "Ellie? What's going on out there?"

Crouching down behind the sofa with Ellie, arms crossed over my head, I explain it as quickly as I can. "Antonio is outside the house trying to shoot us!"

"Stay where you are," he tells us. "Stay down!"

The window in the bedroom opens, and I hear him climbing out.

The next few minutes were tense ones. Ellie and I barely breathed.

"How did you know?" she whispered to me at one point.

I had a dream, I almost tell her, but I realize how mad that's going to sound. "Ellie," I say instead, "you and my son are a perfect couple. I'm happy that he's got you in his life."

"That's what I was going to ask you just now," she says, a little surprised…"Doesn't seem like the time now."

In the dim lighting I found her hand and held it tight in mine. "It's always the right time to ask a mother about her son, when you're in love with the man."

We waited in silence after that. I could hear my own heart beating in my ears. In the excitement my unicorn necklace had fallen outside of my nightshirt and I can see it hanging loose, dangling from my neck.

Thanks, Jess.

We both tensed when we heard the door opening, but it's only Kevin, using the spare key and not breaking it in like I had seen happening in my dream. He's got his gun in one hand and nothing more on than his trousers. Rubbing a hand through his bed-mussed hair, he shrugs. "I can see footprints round the house, but he's gone." He looked over at the broken window, then follows the path the bullet took with his eyes until he finds the hole in the wall. "Lucky for him. If I'd found him out there I might've killed him myself."

I believe him. I know that look. His father used to get that look on his face whenever he'd made his mind up about something. Especially when it involved taking care of his family.

Too bad his father isn't here now to see the man Kevin has grown into. He'd be proud.

I know I am.

⌒

When I finally checked the time I found it was only three-thirty in the morning. Ellie had been right. It was too early to go out. Or was that something she had said in my dream? I really can't remember which was which anymore. Either way, she was right. Normal people didn't do business at this hour.

Kevin had his own objections about me going out, knowing there was a madman killer taking potshots at me. Trying to get rid of witnesses now, I guess. Might be best if I left town, was what Kevin told me. Go to see the rellies up in Sydney.

I talked him into a compromise. I was still going to do exactly what I wanted to do, but he could come with me.

It was just about an hour later when I sat in the front seat of Kevin's car and he and Ellie said their goodbyes on the porch. We were all dressed and ready to go, but Ellie was in her overcoat and pulling her suitcase behind her as well. I felt bad, messing up their visit, even though it wasn't really my fault. They'd both smiled at me in that way people do when they're being understanding, but I knew they regretted losing even a few hours together.

Kevin wasn't letting me out of his sight but he had some private things to say to his girlfriend that a mom probably shouldn't listen in on. Fair enough.

I couldn't hear what they said, but I could tell by the look in their eyes and the way her fingers touched his face that it was personal, and it was intense. That's what love looked like. I remembered having the same thing with Kevin's father. If he'd found that sort of love with Ellie, then I meant every word I'd said to her about the two of them. Even if I had said most of it in a dream.

That was weird, that bit. Waking up, talking to Ellie and interacting with the world around me, only to wake up again to realize it had been a dream. Only, not a dream. Had Jess sent me a warning? Had she really been there—as a spirit, I mean—or could ghosts enter people's dreams, or…

Yeah. I had a lot of questions that needed answering about all of that. Maybe another call to Darcy Sweet would answer some of it for me. When I had time.

Right now, I needed to find out if I was right. Antonio Ferarro, and whoever he worked for, had been tipped off about Torey Walters. I think I have a pretty good idea who did that. Getting him to admit it might be tricky, but it might just save a lot more lives in the process.

Mine included.

With a final kiss and a whispered word, Ellie went off to her car, pulling her wheeled suitcase behind her, looking over her shoulders constantly for fear that some crazy bloke with a gun was about to pop out of the trees. I don't blame her, but I know Antonio isn't out there right now. He tried to strike at us from the shadows and he failed. He'll wait for another chance some other time.

"We need to find Antonio before he tries that again," Kevin says to me as he got into the car to my right, behind the wheel. "I am not going to give him another shot at my mother."

"Exactly what I was thinking." He started the car as I said it and switched on the headlights against the darkness. "If we find his partner, we'll find him."

"You're sure about this?" Kevin asked me. "I mean, that's a pretty big assumption. If he tipped Antonio Ferarro off…"

"Then you arrest him."

"Gonna be a pretty mess in the papers."

I couldn't care less. I just want my family safe, and I want Jess's killer brought to justice. "Just drive," I tell him. "We'll worry about what comes of it after."

"Isn't that what every good Taswegian does?" he joked.

The house he took me to is a humble white bungalow that doesn't stand out from its neighbors. There's flower gardens in front, one to each side of the door, and they display red and blue and yellow blooms in Kevin's headlights. The walkway up to the front door is made of dull black dolerite flagstones like the kind that would come from the quarry where Torey Walters was hiding out. The world's largest supply of that stone is right here in Australia, which makes it pretty easy to come by for construction or yard decoration.

Kevin reached past me to knock on the front door, and then we waited.

Lights came on inside the house, and a curtain moved as someone peeked out. Here we go, I told myself. This is not going to be an easy convo, that's a given. This man has his pride, I'm sure, although you'd never know it from his simple home, or the way he answered the door with a smile.

Or how he's wearing pajama bottoms with dinosaurs on them.

"Dell? Kevin? It's way too early for visitors, don't ya think?"

I looked him straight in his liquid blue eyes. "Sorry, James. This couldn't wait."

James Callahan, reporter extraordinaire for the Lakeshore Times, had been very interested in the death of my friend. He'd been at the police station the day of the search. He had all of the inside information on the crime that I had given him over a lunch that I had thought was just two friends talking.

It was possible that the man was just doing his job.

On the other hand, this could be our killer's inside man.

"We need to talk," Kevin told him. "This is official police business."

James pushed his sandy blonde hair back into place, sort of, and scrunched up his forehead. If it occurred to him he was naked from the waist up, it didn't seem to bother him.

I noticed.

Ahem.

"You always bring your mom along on business, Kevin?" he asked.

"I do when it involves her," was the quick response. "Someone tried to shoot her tonight."

Those words impacted on James, I could tell. There was definitely something going on with him. His eyes darted from Kevin to me. "Are you all right? Did he hurt you?"

"Now, that's interesting," Kevin said.

James blinked at him. "What d'ya mean?"

"Well, you asked if 'he' hurt her. Never said it was a guy who shot at her."

"Was it a woman, then?"

He asked it so innocently that for a moment I thought maybe I was wrong. Maybe he didn't have…no. It had to be him. Who else?

"Let's go inside," Kevin suggested. Then he added, a moment too late, "Please?"

"Of course, of course. Anything to help, if Dell's in trouble." He stepped aside for us, and just like that we were all inside, all the lights in the house switched on, and a kettle boiling on the stove. He excused himself for a moment to change into sweats and a gray t-shirt.

James invited us to sit at the little round kitchen table, four chairs squeezed around it, then spent the next minute or so clearing papers and folders and notebooks away before he sat down with us. "Research," he told us. "On this case, and a few other stories I'm working on. Sorry. I don't usually have company over. Not at this hour."

"We're not company," Kevin told him.

"Yeah. Getting that feeling. Well, you've got my attention. What's going on here, Kevin?"

My son looked over at me, waiting for me to ask the first question. I didn't have the police officer skills that he does. All I knew to do was ask. "James, did you tell anyone that Torey was still in Lakeshore?"

"What?" He shook his head. "I don't understand. I mean, of course I did, I wrote up a whole story on it. It'll be printed in today's paper. Something like this'll be front page material. So?"

"That's not what we're asking." Kevin explained, leaning his elbows on the table. "Did you tell anyone yesterday that we were going to do a search round Lakeshore for Torey Walters? In the quarry?"

"Kevin, I only heard about it from one of the guys down at the fire station." The kettle began to whistle and he got up to get it off the burner. "When I got to the police department you already had twenty people there to do the search. Had no idea where everybody was going, but the whole town knew 'bout it by then."

That was true. In a small town like this, I'd seen gossip spread faster than a wildfire in the bush. Still, for Antonio to be waiting for me at my Inn by the time I got back, someone had to let him know about Torey Walters before the search even got underway. That didn't happen from gossip. Someone who was there must've called him.

"James." My voice had a hard edge to it when I spoke his name. "If you did this, you should know it isn't just me you're putting in danger. This bloke, this Antonio Ferarro, will kill anyone in his way. He killed my friend. He tried to kill me and that bullet could have just as easily hit Kevin or…" I saw my son's face. He still wasn't ready to let that secret out. "…or anyone else."

"Dell, I don't know what you think I…hold on." He paused, kettle in one hand, three mugs with tea bags in them waiting to be filled up. "Did you say Antonio Ferarro?"

"You can't print this, James." Kevin's warning was very clear. "This is all off the record. If you want access to anything the department does, ever again, then I don't see a word of this in the paper."

James stared at him like he'd gone round the bend. "You couldn't stop me if I wanted to print a whole transcript, word for word, of everything ya just said, Kevin. Be that as it may that's not why I'm asking. I know how serious this is. Especially if the likes of Antonio Ferarro's involved. Do ya know who he is?"

"He's the guy trying to kill me," is my answer. "That's all I really need to know."

"No," James assured me. "It's not."

Putting the kettle down in the middle of the stove, he went to the counter where he'd stacked the papers from the table. In the middle of them he found a manila folder.

"This is what ya need to know." He sat down, opening the folder and turning it to me. "I couldn't care less about a byline in this one. Antonio Ferarro's a soldier in the Catalaggi family. They're part of the 'Ndrangheta. It's like the Mafia, only worse."

"I know what the 'Ndrangheta is," Kevin said.

I don't. They were pronouncing it N drawngetta, no matter how it was spelled on the page in front of me, and I sure had no idea what it was. Like the Mafia, only worse? That probably sounded just as bad as it was. "Why do you have a file on him?" I asked.

"It's from the arrest of Roy Fittimer. The drug dealer that Torey Walters was connected to. It's why Torey came to Lakeshore in the first place. Figured it would all connect up in the end. Looks like it is."

I followed his line of reasoning through. Roy had been arrested in a big, splashy, headlines-making arrest as part of the investigation into the poisonings in town last year. He was a drug dealer. One of the biggest in Tasmania. Got noticed by the big boys, these N drawngetta. Torey had been one of his drug runners. When Roy got arrested, Torey was left without a paycheck.

So, she'd stolen money from the mob. No, not the mob. Worse than the mob. She stole money from the 'Ndrangheta and ran right back here.

Then she called Jess for help. They knew each other from before, back when they were both working girls. Organized crime had their fingers in prostitution just like they did in drug trafficking. Torey Walters had been in bed—no pun intended—with organized crime, stole from them, and then nearly lost her life because of it.

Instead, she'd gotten my friend killed.

"So Antonio's a hitman for the mob," Kevin was saying, flipping through the pages in the folder.

"Yes," James said. "Made quite a name for himself, too. Got a reputation for doing jobs in high rises. Likes to leap from ledge to ledge, get into places where the front door's locked. That sort of thing."

"That's bad, no denying," I said. "Still don't explain who tipped him off."

"You think I…" James sat back in his chair, blowing out a breath. "Dell, I'd never do that to you. To anyone. I haven't been talking to ya just for the info. I really did care. Do care," he corrected. "That day, in the Milkbar, I really was just a friend."

Okay, color me a fool, but I believed him. There's a look in his eyes, same as before, and I understand it now. I haven't seen that look in a man's eyes in a long while, but there's no imagining it's anything but what it is.

He didn't tip off Antonio. Someone else did, but it wasn't James. Who?

"Dell," he says, his voice quiet and withdrawn, "I, uh, want to say something to ya. Um."

Kevin's mobile rings, saving James from trying to put his feelings into words. I can't tell if I'm relieved or disappointed.

"Hello." Kevin stands up with the call. Then after a long few seconds, he swears. I didn't know he even knew some of those words. "You have got to be kidding me. No. No, don't do that. I'll be right there."

He hung up, and turned to me, his face angry, his voice tight.

"Torey Walters is dead."

CHAPTER THIRTEEN

Kevin brought me with him to the police station. James offered to let me stay with him, but Kevin wanted me where he could see me and keep me safe. I didn't argue. Mostly, because I didn't want to bring the same trouble to James's doorstep that I'd brought to my own son's.

Mostly.

We weren't two steps inside the front door to the police station when we heard Cutter yelling.

"Guess he doesn't like to be woke up out of bed either," Kevin said to me in a low voice. I doubt he needed to whisper. At the moment Cutter was loving the sound of his own voice too much. "Come on, then."

He used his key to get us through the door to the inner office space, and then told me to take a seat out in the radio dispatch area until he'd told Cutter I was with him. Considering that Lakeshore's Senior Sergeant had already thrown me out of the building once this week, and arrested Kevin out of spite a few days before that, waiting here seemed like a good plan.

I could hear Kevin knock on the door to Cutter's office. I counted ten seconds off in my head before I heard the reaction.

"What! Why in the name of all that is holy do ya keep bringing that woman here! Strike a light! What do ya think this is, bush week?"

It went on like that for a while. Spinning in the little office chair, I let him blow off his steam.

This building has never seemed so small as it does today. I can't believe all of this is happening. First Jess, now Torey Walters. My hands start shaking as I remember my name could've been added to that list. I was the only one who had seen Antonio's face and could identify him for who he was…

No. I wasn't the only one.

Oh, God forgive me, why hadn't I realized this sooner?

I jumped out of my chair and ran for the door, meaning to run all the way back to the Inn if I had to, only to stop and turn back, knowing I have to tell Kevin first. I'm going to need his help.

Rosie. Rosie had seen Antonio's face. She was with me when we hid in the Inn, and Antonio spoke to her. He asked her to make a raspberry tart, for the love of God!

"I wasn't watching her!" I hear Cutter yelling. "Blake had guard duty. At his house. I want him arrested! I want the bludger in handcuffs, in my cell, before the sun comes up! I don't give a rat's—"

My bad luck to open the door in the middle of that sentence.

Cutter's face was already crimson, veins standing out on his neck. Kevin and one other officer were standing, weathering the storm of their Senior Sergeant's anger, but I could see how uncomfortable they were to be in this room. When he turned the heat of his glare on me, I came very close to shoving it back down his throat. It was my friend who had died, not his, and if he'd only listened to me and Kevin from the start of this then we wouldn't be standing where we are today!

"This is a private discussion!" he bellowed at me, louder than a herd of bull elephants. "You do not come into my office unless I say—!"

"Stuff it, Cutter!" I snapped, knowing it's exactly the wrong thing to say at exactly the wrong time. I actually see the other officer and my son cringe. "Kevin, we need to get to Rosie. Antonio might go after her."

Understanding spread over his face as he caught on. "I should'a thought of that one myself. Senior Sergeant, I have to go. Antonio Ferarro is still out there and my mom's right. If he went after her, he could be going after Rosie, too."

Cutter picked up random files from his desk and tossed them into the air, like a child throwing a tantrum. "Well that's just crash hot, then. Go on with ya. I'll just mop up the mess on this end while yer playing follow the leader with yer mom! Tell me the truth, Powers. I woulda been better off to hire her, wouldn't I?"

Smarter than his years, Kevin didn't rise to the bait.

A little less wiser for my years, I started to say something that probably would have gotten Kevin fired. He grabbed me by my wrist and pulled me physically out of the room before I could, saving us both the embarrassment of learning whether I could shout Cutter down.

I could. I know I could.

"Not the best of plans, Mom," Kevin says to me when we're outside and getting back into his car. "If you want me to stay on this case, best not to upset the apple cart too much."

"Cutter's as bad an apple as they come," I point out. "And I don't care about his ego. I only care about Rosie being safe."

"Did you try calling her?"

"Rang her mobile. There's no answer. She might even be at the Inn already, starting breakfast."

His car roared to life and he spun it around in the street to head it back toward town. "Then why don't you just call the Inn?"

"Because at this hour all of the incoming calls get sent up to my phone. No one would even know I was calling."

"Great system," Kevin grumbled. "Add that to the list of things to change, right after putting alarms on your windows."

"We'll need to split up." Okay, for the record, I don't like that plan. In fact, I hate it, but I don't see any other way. Cutter won't be able to spare any men. One of his officers is already driving me across town at top speed and he intends to arrest another. All we have is each other. "Drop me off at the end of Fenlong Street. I can check the Inn, you can check her house."

"I'm not doing that. No way."

"Kevin, this is my friend. My best friend. I've already lost Jess. I can't…I can't lose Rosie."

We turn onto Fenlong Street with a squeal of tires and then a harsh jamming of brakes as the car starts down the slope to the Inn. "I'll take a quick look with you. If she's not there, we'll find her."

I looked at him, wanting a promise.

"We will, mom. We'll find her."

Pulling into the driveway too fast, we kicked up dirt and a flurry of leaves as we skidded to a halt. I was the first one to the door. Kevin was half a step behind me, pulling me back to go in first, gun drawn and ready.

Hard to imagine a quieter place than the Inn at that moment. It was nearing six o'clock, and I could hear a few of my employees moving around out in the kitchen, but other than that and the tick-tock of seconds slipping past us from the clock on the wall, everything was silent. The lights were off in the common room. The sign was up on the desk asking guests to ring my room if they needed anything.

Everything seemed fine.

On our way to the kitchen we met Paul, the young male server who Jess had found so cute, a tray full of dishes bound for the tables here in the dining room. "Heya, Dell. You're up early."

"Is Rosie in?" I asked him, knowing I don't have time for small talk.

"Er, no. Ain't seen her as yet. Kinda early for her. She left us directions for breakfast last night and—"

"I'll check her house," Kevin told me, squeezing my arm before turning to leave. He was trying to be reassuring.

It just wasn't working.

"You mean, we'll check her house," I said, catching up to him.

"No, Mom. Stay here. Rosie walks to work every morning. If she's walking between her house and here, we might miss her altogether. We don't have time to search the whole neighborhood. I'll check her house, you stay here in case she shows up to work."

I don't like this plan, either.

But he's right.

"Lock the door behind me," is his final bit of advice. Then he's gone out into the night, his car speeding back up Fenlong.

Probably a bad time to tell him that these doors haven't had locks for years. Never figured I needed locks on doors that were always open to guests.

Sure. I know. One more thing to add to the list of changes to make when this was over.

"Dell?" I heard Paul asking behind me. "What's going on?"

"Seen anyone come into the Inn?" I asked him. He's still got that tray of dishes in his hands and his eyes are nearly as wide as the saucers.

"Guests have all been in bed. Nobody's up and moving except the hired help. Me and the others in the kitchen. Ain't even seen George yet. He's usually in by now." He follows me to the doors. "Something's wrong, ain't it?"

Closing the doors won't keep anyone out, not without a lock, but at least we'll have some warning if they get opened. They're heavy pine wood, no windows, and I doubt even a hired killer for the 'Ndrangheta would start taking blind shots through a door.

"Paul." I finally turn my attention on him, knowing that I have to tell him something. "Get all of the servers and the cooks into the kitchen. Stay there until you hear from me or from Kevin. Understand?"

He nodded his head at the same time that he said, "Er, no."

"But you'll do what I ask?"

"Sure thing."

"Good. See me tomorrow about a raise."

"Really?" A smile settled on his face and he hands the tray of dishes to me so he can run back to the kitchen and tell everyone what I needed them to do.

I set the tray down on the registration desk. Antonio's hat and note are gone, taken as evidence by Kevin to put in the growing file surrounding Jess's death. "Didn't know you were going to cause all this uproar, did you Jess?" I felt for the unicorn necklace on the cord around my neck, and I can't help but laugh. "'Course, you always did cause a scene wherever you went."

The feeling of fingertips brushing against the back of my neck makes me turn around. No one is there.

I guess there's nothing for me to do now but wait.

Trying Rosie's cell phone twice more doesn't do anything. Just a busy signal again, both times. "Come on, Rosie. Where are you?"

I start pacing just for something to do. I know it won't take Kevin long to check on Rosie's house and get back here. It just feels like it's taking forever. I exhaust the foyer pretty quickly, then move on to pace into the common room. It's dark in there. We keep the lights off at night when they're aren't any guests watching television or playing cards.

Twenty paces from registration desk to the sitting couch, and twenty paces back. I know the whole Inn like the back of my hand, and I know where to step each time, because there won't be anything here that I'm not expecting.

Except that.

On the floor is a little square of waxed paper. A small and brightly colored candy wrapper.

Oh, snap.

"Sorry," Antonio said to me from the darkness. "I know it's impolite of me to litter like that. I'll clean it up later, I will."

When he stood up I saw him, finally, melting out of the shadows where he'd been sitting and into the light. He's dressed just like before, maybe even in the same clothes, with his suitcoat and white button-up shirt left open at his neck, his tie hanging loose. "Actually," he said, "that's a lie. I've cleaned up more'n me share of messes in this podunk town. Got me one more mess to take care of. After this, I'm done."

Had he been sitting here this whole time? Watching me from the dark? A shudder ran down my spine as he came right over to where I stood, and I wanted to run, but somehow I knew if I turned my back on this man, I'd be dead.

With a twisted smile, Antonio took my chin in his hand. "I know there's people over in that kitchen. Don't be calling for help. You have to die because you saw me face. That's just the way it is. Torey Walters is already dead, from what I hear. That Rosie woman's gonna have to go, too, but after that nobody else needs to get hurt. Less'n you involve someone else. Just you two fine ladies, then I pick up the fifty thousand that Torey stole from us, and I'm gone. I was gonna wait for the two of you's to be here, but…" He shrugged, like it was no matter to him when we died. "So. Let's just leave this between me and you, shall we?"

I nod my head, seeing the lethal intent in his eyes, and I'm very sure he means every word he just said. He's going to kill me. He's going to kill Rosie. Then he'll be gone like the wind, leaving only dust in his wake.

Which meant Rosie is still alive! Thank God for small miracles. Kevin would find her and keep her safe, at least.

One other thing he said is what really catches my interest. He knew Torey was dead, from what he heard. He didn't do it himself, and there hadn't been time for that tidbit to hit the rumor mill yet. We only found out two hours ago from Senior Sergeant Cutter himself. When we were at James's place. Kevin had gotten that phone call and then told me what had happened while James sat there, listening…

James.

I'll kill him. I'll break his neck myself with my own two hands! I believed him when he said he hadn't told hitman Antonio anything. Liar! James must've called him right after we left his house.

I will kill him. All by myself with my two little hands. That's a promise.

If I make it out of here alive, that is.

"Let's step outside," Antonio says to me now. "Me and you can go round back, into the trees down by the lake, where it's nice and quiet and no one else needs to see us, how's that sound?"

There is no way I want to go anywhere with this man. I know what's at the end of that walkabout. But I wasn't going to be responsible for anyone else being put in danger. I couldn't do that to the people who worked for me. My guests. Everyone else in town for that matter.

So I let him push me out the front doors and into the half-light of predawn.

Once we were outside, Antonio pulled out a slim automatic pistol that glinted a metallic silver. From inside his suitcoat he took out a black cylinder that he proceeded to screw into the barrel of the gun.

A silencer.

Death in Room 7

When it was attached he waved the tip of it at the corner of the Inn closest to the shoreline.

I couldn't breathe. Couldn't hear anything except the booming echo of my own heart. My legs trembled and my knees were weak as I took one step after the other, around to the back of the building.

Just past the corner is a heap of something that I nearly step on before I realize it's a man. Laying on his back, eyes closed, head rolled to the side, is George. My handyman. Blood is a dark splotch below his left ear, and it might have been the weak lighting or just my imagination, but his skin was very pale.

I covered my mouth with both hands, sure that a scream is about to come burbling up out of me.

"Relax," Antonio chuckled. "He'll be right as rain. Got a hard head, this one. Managed to bash it a good one before he saw me. So. No need to waste a bullet on him. Don't you wish I could say the same 'bout you?"

Poor George. All he ever wanted to do was help people. He loved working at the Inn. I couldn't ask for a more dedicated worker, or friend.

"Move," Antonio reminded me. "Down there."

As we go, I take a good look at the Inn. My life's work. The realization of a dream for both me and Rosie. I picked out that color of yellow, so different from the white of every other building in town, and argued with Mayor Brown to get the permission to keep it that way. I had overseen every bit of the renovations to the place. Chosen each employee along with Rosie. Agonized over every decision that had built the business up to where it was right now.

Even down to placing the little storage building out back.

Antonio gestured with the gun at the trees over by the lake. "Down there, I think."

I don't think so. Down there, I'm a dead woman. I have another idea entirely.

I want to live.

Without warning I break and run. Not for the safety of the trees. Not for the solid security of the Inn that had been my home for years. I don't try to cut across lots to the nearest houses either, a few hundred yards away.

The little storage shed is my destination.

"Hey!" is all Antonio managed to get out before I'm at the door to the shed and wrenching it open. I hear the faint *thwip thwip* of gunshots muted through the silencer as I throw myself inside. I don't know where the bullets went, and I don't have time to find out.

I've got a madman on my heels.

"You're a dead woman," Antonio hissed at me into the silence of the night. "Get back here!"

Inside the shed, I found exactly what I was looking for.

"You hear me?" Antonio demanded. "I said get out here, right now!"

Well. He asked for it.

Pedaling as hard as I can I flew out of the shed on the Wallaby right into the path of Mister Antonio Ferarro, hired hitman. The ten-speed's front tire caught him in the chest with a little help from a balancing act I haven't tried since I was ten. The wheelie maneuver probably looked cooler than it felt, and the jarring impact nearly unseated me, but it drove him to the ground and I was on my way.

The knobby tires on my bicycle eat up the ground and bring me right around to Fenlong Street.

Just in time for Kevin's car to come wheeling into the driveway.

I've never been so happy to see anyone before in my life. He stopped just short of me, and I spun my bicycle around so that I'm at his window. Gesturing, panting for breath because I'm scared out of my wits, I pointed back in the direction of the backyard. "He's there! He's right there!"

And he was. Antonio Ferarro had followed me, up from the beating my Wallaby had given him, gun still in hand, aiming it straight at me.

There are moments in your life when you are so completely terrified that you can't move. I knew I was going to die in that instant. I knew it with a certainty that froze every muscle in my body.

I...could...not...move.

Thankfully there was someone else watching over me.

A shadow stood suddenly between us. The dark shape of a woman I was proud to call my friend, despite her secrets.

Jessica turned and winked at me. It's just a faint impression of that pretty face of hers, caught between the faint light of approaching dawn and the headlights of Kevin's car, and the dark expression on Antonio's face.

"You," I heard him growl. "It can't be you. You're dead!"

"Who's he talking to?" Kevin wondered out loud as he clambered out of his car, gun drawn, ready for anything. Well. Anything but this.

"Don't you see her?" I asked him.

"See...who? Mom, there's no one there."

Jess laughed.

I could see it as plain as anything, and it broke my heart because this was my friend. This was the happy-go-lucky girl that I had known at University standing here in the way of danger meant for me. The friend I would never see again.

I watched, as she turned and blurred at Antonio in a streak of movement that blended into the first true rays of sunlight streaking down from above. Antonio screamed in a very unmanly way and squeezed the trigger on his gun, once.

The bullet is quiet as it leaves the extended barrel. When it hits the hood of Kevin's car it makes an impossibly loud metallic *thwunk*.

Kevin was shouting at me to get down as he took aim with his own gun and fired two rounds in quick succession. Jess was already gone as the rounds stuck a shocked Antonio, slamming him backward, off his feet, to the ground.

As Kevin raced over to the wounded hitman I took ahold of the unicorn necklace, just to feel the little pendant in my hand. Jess just saved my life. Kevin's too, maybe.

While he twisted Antonio's body around and dropped handcuffs onto the man's wrists—not gently—I said a quiet thanks to a friend who stood by me when I needed her most, even after death.

My tears mixed with a smile.

This was finally over.

CHAPTER FOURTEEN

"Mom, he was just blinded by the sun. There wasn't anyone there."

Kevin had sung this tune all morning, and I've decided to just stop arguing with him about it. Smiling sweetly, I poured him more coffee, and then offered him the sugar bowl.

"Black is fine, thanks." He rubbed at his tired eyes. "I've got to get back to the station. Cutter's in a fine mood, I tell you what."

"Cutter can kiss my—"

"Mom!"

"Well, he can." I drank more of my own coffee, then put the cup down firmly on the table we're sitting at in the dining room of the Inn. We had to shut the whole place down for a few hours, so I had the servers run breakfast trays up to the guests in their rooms, and then sent most of them home. The Inn is a crime scene once again. Nobody was allowed to come in who wasn't already here.

George was all right, thank God. Just unconscious like Antonio had said. He had quite the bump to the back of his noggin and a possible concussion on top of it, so it was off to the medical center in Geeveston for him. His statement to Kevin had been pretty short.

"Something hit me from behind."

They'd shared a laugh about that as the rescue squad members strapped him to a gurney and loaded him into their white rig with its yellow and red stripes to drive him away to hospital. I was happy to know he'd be okay.

Antonio Ferarro was another matter entirely.

Kevin's two shots had both bit deeply into the man's right shoulder. There had been a lot of blood lost, and I heard one of the EMTs say something about a broken bone, but they'd missed his heart. I was impressed. "That was a dead-on bit of shooting, cowboy," I had joked with Kevin.

I'll always remember the scowl on his face when he told me he'd missed. Turns out he'd been aiming center mass, and Antonio had moved.

Lucky for him. Lucky for Kevin, too. I'm just as glad he didn't have to live with someone's death on his conscience. Even someone like Antonio Ferarro, hitman for the 'Ndrangheta.

The other officers from the Lakeshore PD had been over the Inn from top to bottom while all this other stuff was going on, collecting the candy wrappers as evidence of Antonio's involvement in Jess's death and taking statements from wide-eyed guests.

"You know, my Inn is getting quite the reputation," I mutter.

"Gonna hurt your business?" Kevin asked.

"Hardly. Half the people I have staying here now have booked reservations already for next year. Guess they like the excitement."

"Ha. Crazy tourists," Kevin smiles. "Don't they know people come to Lakeshore to relax? Nothing exciting ever happens here."

I raise my coffee cup to that, and we clink the ceramic mugs together in a toast to our beloved town. We may not have been born here, but it really has become home to both of us.

"Here we go!" Rosie said brightly as she swept in from the kitchen. "Lamingtons with strawberry jam and cream and chocolate icing."

She had apologized to me over and over, when she finally got here, for being late. Her cell phone had died and her husband had forgotten to set the alarm, and somewhere around that part of the very long explanation she broke down in tears and retreated to the kitchen. She'd been in there baking ever since, for the guests and, apparently, for us too.

In Rosie's world, food made just about anything better.

She was okay. That was what mattered to me. She was safe, and I was safe, and Kevin was, too. The bad guy was in handcuffs. All things considered, I suppose it was the best we could hope for.

Rosie set the three plates down, one for each of us. She sat down to join us and then folded her hands in front of her. "Lord, thank you for bringing us all to this moment, safe and sound and able to enjoy good food. Amen."

I watched her. When she noticed, she paused with a forkful of lamington halfway to her mouth. "What?"

"Nothing. I just don't remember you ever saying grace before."

She looked a little embarrassed as she took the bite of food from her fork and then talked around it. "Well, I figure with all we've been through it won't hurt to thank the Lord above. Ya have to admit, it's been a week we'd all rather forget."

I couldn't argue with that. Maybe I'd even stop in to hear Pastor Albright's sermon this Sunday. First Jess, then Torey, now all of this here at the Inn this morning. Which reminded me.

"What did they find out about Torey's death?" I asked Kevin. Hard to believe I hadn't thought of asking this before, but with everything else going on here, that poor girl's death had been pretty far down my list of things to worry about.

It's a pretty long list.

Kevin's face turned sour and he pushed aside his uneaten pastry. "Didn't find out anything good, I'm sorry to say. Blake Williams had guard duty on her when she turned up dead. Cutter had put her in Blake's house for safekeeping til we figured out what to do with her.

So there she is, tucked away all safe. Blake's supposed to be keeping his eye on her. Only, he says he heard a noise off in the trees outside. Went to investigate, came back, and Torey had been strangled to death."

"Poor girl," Rosie said, crossing herself.

"Do you believe him?" I had to ask. With everything else that happened it was awfully convenient that Torey would just up and die. "Do you think he's telling the truth?"

"Well, any other time I'd say yes." Kevin crossed his arms, staring down at the table. After a moment he just shook his head. "Thing is, that's not the end of it. Senior Sergeant Cutter went through Blake's house, and found the money Torey had taken from the crime family. All thirty thousand of it. Hidden under the floorboards."

I let that sink in. Blake Williams had always been a bit of a dunce, and he trailed along behind Cutter like a dog licking at his master's heels…but killing? Well. I suppose thirty thousand dollars would be enough motive for some. Not for me, not by a long shot, but I guess there's always people willing to sell their soul for that much. Judas sold his for thirty pieces of silver after all. I guess if you adjusted for inflation…

Wait.

"How much did you say?" My mind was replaying something from my memory, something that Antonio Ferarro had said to me this morning. "Cutter found the money?"

"Well, sure," Blake shrugged.

"And he found how much?"

"That's not really your business, is it?" Cutter himself said, sauntering in with a stony glare aimed at Kevin. "That'd be police business, and not a matter to share with civilians, now ain't that right, Officer Powers?"

Kevin stood up from the table after giving me an apologetic look. "Absolutely, Senior Sergeant. Sorry. I was just—"

"Telling stories outta turn." He pointed with his finger back to the lobby and the front door. "Why don't ya head back to the station with the others. We got a lot to sort out, and yer mommy ain't part of any of it."

I bristled at the way he said that. Kevin's jaw clenched as he gave a tight nod and stepped out without looking back. He must've figured he had me in enough trouble already. I didn't care about that. I was thinking about something else entirely. Cutter's eyes locked on mine, and I could see him reading my thoughts.

"What?" he growled.

Rosie felt the tension between us. She popped up out of her seat and grabbed the half-finished plates of lamington, shifting them in her hands and threatening to spill them all over as she backed her way toward the kitchen. "Uh, I'll get things started for the lunch service, Dell. If ya don't need me?"

She didn't really wait for an answer before disappearing behind the swinging kitchen door.

Then it was just me, and Angus Cutter.

"Something ya want to say?" he demanded, leaning his hands against the back of the chair Kevin had been sitting in.

I looked up at him, and I knew. Without any question, I knew.

"It was you," I told him.

A little smirk curled his lips. "You're gonna have to be more specific."

I planted my hands on the tabletop and pushed myself up. I was shorter than him, though not by much, but I stared him in the eye with all the righteous anger that five-feet-seven inches could manage.

He backed away a step.

"You tipped off the 'Ndrangheta." All this time I had thought it was James. I had thought awful things about James, sure that it was him who had gotten my friend killed and put me and Rosie and Kevin in danger. But it hadn't been him after all.

It was Cutter.

"You're daft," he said to me now, that infuriating half-smile still in place and mocking me. "I know you've been through a lot, but I wouldn't go making accusations you'll never prove."

"It was you," I say again, reading the truth in his eyes. "You told Antonio Ferarro where to find me, this morning here at the Inn. You killed Torey yourself!"

"Oh, really? And just how do ya know that?"

"Because Antonio said he was looking for fifty thousand dollars, not thirty."

The color drained from his face and that stupid grin turned feral. He jabbed a finger at me, but kept his distance. "Got all the answers, don't ya? Well, then answer me this. If'n I did that, why wouldn't I take all the money? Huh? Why would I bother killing that whore at all?"

Some of the wind slipped out of my sails. I hadn't thought about the why, just the who.

I suppose the first question was easy enough to answer. He couldn't take all of the money for himself, because the mob would come looking for it. If he had most of the money in evidence, no one would dare touch it. Hard to walk into a police station and complain your illegally obtained cash was missing a few bills.

The other thing he'd said, though…that was trickier. Why would he kill her? Why not just rob her and turn her loose? Or confiscate the money and skim off his twenty grand then, leaving Torey alive.

Why?

If Antonio had killed Torey, he would have taken all the money with him. And Blake was stupid, but not stupid enough to kill a girl and then set himself up to be arrested for it. That left Cutter as the only suspect.

But…why?

My mind raced through possibilities. What I settled on, as the most likely reason, was that Torey had known something Cutter couldn't risk anyone else hearing. Something to do with him. Something serious enough that he was willing to kill to cover it up, and then frame one of his own officers to take the blame.

Which was a great theory, except what was it that Torey had known?

I didn't know the answer to that.

This time, it was me who backed down. I looked away from him, from those eyes and their anger and their deep darkness. I was seeing him in a different way now. He'd always been an incompetent glory hound. Could he be something much worse?

That whole mess with Roy Fittimer the drug dealer came back to mind. Cutter had kept that whole investigation under wraps for months before my friend Darcy Sweet had blown it wide open. The excuse Cutter gave at the time had been that he was tailing Fittimer through a host of drug deals and illegal activity to find the bigger fish the man worked for. All the while, Fittimer had dealt drugs right here in Lakeshore and across the southern states.

What if Cutter hadn't arrested Fittimer because he was in on it? Taking a portion of the illegal sales to line his own pocket? What if it had nothing to do with good police work, and everything to do with Cutter's own greed?

Just like the twenty thousand he'd stolen from Torey.

And maybe that was what Torey knew.

Cutter blew me a kiss. "If I was you, Dell, I'd be a might careful about accusing someone of being in bed with the 'Ndrangheta.

Especially the Senior Sergeant of police. Until there was some proof for your wild accusations."

With a nasty laugh, he turned, and walked out of my Inn.

My skin crawled. What was I going to do about Cutter? As much as I hated to admit it, he was right. Without proof, I might as well be spitting into the wind. All the maybes and what-ifs in the world didn't amount to a hill of sand. He'd get away with what he'd done if I started throwing around accusations before I could back them up.

I couldn't prove anything.

At least, not yet.

⁓

It was a few hours more before I got everything situated at the Inn and felt comfortable leaving again. I had to reassure the guests that everything was all right, and then the Carpenters wanted to book two more return stays. They were wide-eyed at all the goings on and even said their friends were asking for the phone number so they could book a weekend here at the Pine Lake Inn. I guess death and intrigue are what the people want.

There were servers to get back on task. Menus to plan. Rooms to reopen—Jess's included—and arrangements to make for…

Yeah. All of that is pretty much a lie.

I was finding busy work to do. It wasn't that I didn't feel comfortable leaving the Inn again. I was avoiding going out for an entirely different reason.

Walking over to James Callahan's house again only took me twenty minutes or so. Kind of dragged my feet, but I got there eventually, stood on his porch, and knocked on his door. Part of me was hoping that maybe he was at the office reporting the big news.

Just my luck. The man has a job that lets him work from home.

"Heya, Dell. I was just filing my story by e-mail," he said to me after answering the door with a tired smile. "Give me five minutes and I'll have it submitted. Unless ya have something I can add to it?"

Cutter's a thief, I almost said. Senior Sergeant Cutter's a full on lowlife who might be a murderer and the whole town should ride him out on a rail. That sounded better in my head than I knew it would look in print. Best to keep my mouth closed.

Until I had proof.

"No," I said with an empty smile. "Nothing to add."

"Not sure I believe ya, Dell." He studied me for a moment and then shrugged. "Guess a woman needs to keep some of her secrets. Come on in. Keep me company while I put this one to bed."

I followed him into the living room, where he had a steaming cup of coffee on the end table and his laptop open to a word document. He asked me if I'd like a coffee but I just wanted to get his over so I declined the offer. He sat down immediately and began typing. I sat in one of the two easy chairs and waited, my hands on my knees to keep them from fidgeting.

I watched him as he typed. It was interesting, to see him working. There was something about seeing him that way, so intense, so focused. Made him seem more like himself, somehow. It was attractive on him.

With a flourish and a few more taps, he shut the laptop and set it beside him on the couch. "So. You've had an interesting morning."

"Interesting week," I corrected him. How many days had it been since Jess had arrived in Lakeshore? I wasn't even sure any more. "I, uh, wanted to have a little talk with you."

He sipped at his coffee and raised one eyebrow at me. "Oh? What about?"

Not going to make this easy on me, now was he? "I was thinking some awful things about you. Terrible things. None of them were true, and I feel terrible about it."

Putting the mug aside, he shrugs. "This the bit about thinking I tipped off Antonio Ferarro? Like Kevin and you was asking before?"

I rolled my eyes to the side and nodded as I bit at my lower lip. "I'm sorry."

"Heh, is that all?"

He made it sound like all I did was accuse him of taking the last cookie. "Isn't that enough?"

With a smile and a little shake of his head he took my hand and stood me up again. "The way I figure it," he said, "ya had every reason to be jumpy. A good friend wouldn't hold that against ya."

Before all this started, I had barely known James. Now I couldn't imagine going back to not knowing him like I do. "Is that what we are?" I asked him. "Good friends?"

For a long moment he didn't speak, didn't move, and for all I know he didn't breathe.

Then he leaned in very close to me, and gently kissed my lips.

"I hope maybe more than friends," he said, in a smoky voice.

In that moment, my voice failed me altogether. I think I said something, I'm sure I said something, I just can't remember for the life of me what it was. Something witty, I hope. Something full of half-spoken promises. Or maybe I just mumbled thanks before I turned and beat a path out of his door.

I really hadn't expected that. It was good to know that my instincts had been right about him after all. He was a good man. An honest man. No matter what I'd suspected him of.

A man I could trust to be my friend.

I just hadn't expected…that.

Death in Room 7

On my way home my fingers strayed to my lips. I could still feel the way his mouth had pressed against mine. So warm. So comfortable. Like a first kiss should be.

I might not have expected it, but I certainly enjoyed it. After all, time moves on. It had been a while since I'd let a man into my life.

Maybe it was time for me to move on, too.

CHAPTER FIFTEEN

It was two days later when George was back to work.

And the first thing he did was figure out how to put that painting up in our lobby.

Now, I don't know what George's fascination is with Lieutenant Governor David Collins, but I have to admit his solution was almost elegant in its simplicity.

"There," he said to me when it was done. "How d'ya like it, Dell?"

The man just got back from a stay in the hospital for a concussion and a fractured skull, understand, so at this point I would have let him hang the painting with duct tape if he really wanted to.

Thankfully it didn't come to that.

From the registration desk I looked over at the painting, set up on the floor on its tripod easel, and gave a tip of my head to old David Collins, and George the handyman. "Looks right fine to me. Don't know what you plan on doing with your time now that you've got that squared away."

"Heh. Place like this? Always something needs doing."

He stepped away, whistling to himself, and I found myself agreeing with him. There was always something going on at the Pine Lake Inn.

In a lot of ways.

Things are almost back to normal here now, with a few exceptions.

Jess's room has a new rug in it, and a new chair to boot. The walls have been scrubbed, the bedding changed out. There's no evidence to be found that a good friend died there. I'll still never be able to call it room seven again. It will always be Jess's room to me.

I've had people call up specifically requesting to stay in that room. Part of me is disgusted every time someone asks. Another part of me thinks it's a pretty fair tribute to her. So in the end, I make the reservations. It's more popular now than my honeymoon suite.

Wait until Jess gets a load of that.

I see her still, sometimes, out of the corner of my eye. A slim ghostly figure with long blonde hair, wearing ripped jeans and a t-shirt and laughing over some little thing that someone has said. She'll always be a part of the Inn, now, and a part of my life.

The thing is, I don't think she's the only one.

Now that I've accepted Jess's spirit as a real thing, I kind of get the feeling there are other ghosts in this building. I've felt things, seen things, long before Jess came to Lakeshore. The way nothing stays on that wall, whether it's a painting of David Collins or a clock or a hand-drawn notice on a piece of paper. The way the phone will ring and then crackle with static when no one's there, and then the way you can almost make out words in all that white noise.

The way my skin will creep with cold prickles when I think someone's watching me but all I can see are shadows.

If this Inn really is haunted from events in its past, before me and Rosie took it over, maybe Jess has opened my eyes to see it. Maybe there's always been more to life than what I knew. Who knows? Maybe the next time the phone rings—

I nearly jump out of my skin when the phone on the desk does exactly that, the little red light letting me know it's an outside call coming in.

Laughing at myself I pick up the receiver to answer. "G'day, Pine Lake Inn."

"Why, hello my dear. Would Dell Powers be available to speak to?"

The man's voice on the line is smooth as silk. Or, oily as butter, I suppose. There's an accent, too, one I can't quite place. "This is Dell Powers. Can I help you?"

"I certainly hope so. It would seem we have a lot in common."

Yeah, I don't like the way he said that. "I'm sorry, who am I speaking to?"

"Manners, yes, of course. First, let me tell you why I'm calling. An associate of mine is sitting in jail. Because of you."

Because of...oh. "You mean Antonio Ferarro."

"The very same, my dear."

Oh, snap. "Which makes you, what? Part of the 'Ndrangheta crime family?"

When he chuckles it's like nails on a chalkboard. It makes my skin crawl. "You could say that about me, yes. I'm more of a family patriarch, I suppose you could say. My name is Joseph Catalaggi. I was most upset to hear what befell Antonio."

I finally have enough presence of mind to check the caller ID for the number this Catalaggi fellow is calling from. The little screen just reads, unknown caller. "Mister Catalaggi, your business associate Antonio killed a good friend of mine. He tried to kill me, and other people too. What do you want from me?"

"Want? Why, my dear, I want nothing from you." That soft laugh again. "I only wanted you to know that we are aware of you. Oh, and your son as well. The amazing policeman, Kevin Powers.

Death in Room 7

Took down Roy Fittimer. Arrested Antonio. Busy man, your son. At any rate, I simply wanted to introduce myself, and let you know that we will be in touch. Goodbye, Miss Powers."

Then he hung up.

I held the phone in my hand for a moment, staring at it. Was that a threat? Or an introduction? I felt for the unicorn necklace and held the little pendant tightly.

I had the feeling I'd be hearing from Joseph Catalaggi again.

As I went to replace the receiver, to hang up on that weird call, the phone rang again. The red light didn't blink. It just rang.

It couldn't possibly be ringing. I hadn't put it down yet.

Ring, ring.

I put the phone back to my ear, wondering what was wrong with the thing. "Hello?"

A burst of static filled the line.

I thought I heard something, faint and indistinct.

I'm here.

It wasn't Jess's voice.

But then, who?

Carefully, I hung up the receiver, and stepped away from the desk.

The phone rang again almost immediately.

I was halfway to picking it up again when I decided I needed to check on what Rosie was doing in the kitchen.

There would be time enough for another good mystery tomorrow.

-The End-

RECIPES

JUMBUCK STEW

TOTAL TIME: 15 min
Prep: 20 min
Cook: 1hr 30min
YIELD: 4 servings
LEVEL: Easy

INGREDIENTS

- 1 kg chops (lamb)
- 2 tbs plain flour
- 1 pinch seasoning *to taste
- 2 tsp curry powder
- 1 1/2 tsp ground ginger
- 2 tbs butter
- 1 onion large sliced
- 2 tbs white vinegar
- 4 tbs Worcestershire sauce
- 4 tbs tomato sauce
- 2 tbs brown sugar
- 1 cup beef stock (liquid)
- 500 g pumpkin peeled chopped

DIRECTIONS

1. Trim chops of any fat.
2. Mix flour with salt and pepper, curry powder and ginger and coat chops.
3. Heat half the butter in a heavy based pan and brown lamb chops on both sides. Remove to a plate.
4. Add remaining butter to pan and cook onion gently until soft. Return lamb to pan.

5. Mix vinegar, sauces, sugar and stock and pour over lamb. Cover and bring to simmer, reduce heat to low and simmer gently for 1 hour.
6. Skim any fat off surface and add pumpkin.
7. Cover and cook for a further 30 minutes or until lamb chops and pumpkin are tender.

NOTES
Can be cooked in a slow cooker as well.

PEA, FETA AND MINT SALAD

TOTAL TIME: 15 min
Prep: 10 min
Cook: 5 min
YIELD: 4 servings
LEVEL: Easy

INGREDIENTS

- 7 ounces fresh shelled peas
- Water, as needed
- 3 tablespoons olive oil
- 1 onion, finely diced
- 2 teaspoons Dijon mustard
- 1 tablespoon red wine vinegar
- 1 tablespoon honey
- Sea salt and freshly cracked black pepper
- 1 1/4 ounces shelled pistachio nuts, coarsely chopped
- 1 large handful fresh mint leaves
- 1 3/4 ounces snow pea leaves or baby English spinach
- 2 3/4 ounces Feta cheese, crumbled

DIRECTIONS

In a medium saucepan, bring salted water to a boil. Blanch the peas in the boiling water until they are just tender and bright green, about 2 minutes. Refresh immediately by plunging them into a bowl of cold water. Drain and reserve the peas.

In a small pan, heat 1 tablespoon of the oil over medium heat. Add the onion, and cook until soft, stirring occasionally, about 5 minutes.

Meanwhile, in a small bowl, whisk together the mustard, the remaining 2 tablespoons olive oil, vinegar and honey, and season with salt and black pepper, to taste.

In a large salad bowl, mix the peas, onions, pistachios, and pour over the dressing. Add the mint and snow pea leaves, and gently toss to coat with dressing. Top the salad with the feta cheese just before serving.

THREE CHEESE MACARONI

This is a very special and rich macaroni made with three kinds of cheese. The shape of the baking pan will affect the outcome. If you like lots of 'crunchy stuff,' use a long, shallow pan. A deeper, narrower pan will yield more of the soft 'insides.'

TOTAL TIME: 1hr 20min
Prep: 10 min
Cook: 1hr 10min
YIELD: 4 servings
LEVEL: Easy

INGREDIENTS

- 1kg macaroni
- 300g grated Swiss cheese
- 300g grated mozzarella cheese
- 300g grated Cheddar cheese
- 1/2 cup (125ml) milk
- Salt to taste
- 1/8 teaspoon onion powder
- 1 pinch garlic powder
- 1/4 teaspoon dried parsley
- 3 tablespoons margarine

DIRECTIONS

Preheat oven to 180 degrees C. Grease a 20x30cm baking dish.

Bring a large pot of lightly salted water to a boil. Add pasta and cook for 8 to 10 minutes or until al dente; drain.

In a large bowl combine macaroni, Swiss, mozzarella and Cheddar and stir until cheeses melt. Stir in milk. Season to taste with salt, onion powder, garlic powder and parsley. Spoon into prepared dish and dot with margarine.

Bake in preheated oven 50 to 60 minutes or until top is crunchy.

RASPBERRY TART

TOTAL TIME: 1hr 35 min
Prep: 15 min
Cook: 1hr 10min
YIELD: 10 servings
LEVEL: Easy

INGREDIENTS

- 1 cup/250 ml milk
- 1/2 vanilla bean, halved lengthwise and seeds scraped
- 3 egg yolks
- 1/4 cup/55 g sugar
- 2 tablespoons flour
- 1 tablespoon framboise (raspberry liqueur)
- 1/4 cup/60 ml heavy cream
- 1 pound/450 g fresh raspberries
- 1 (9-inch/23 cm) prepared baked cookie crust

DIRECTIONS

Put the milk in a saucepan. Split the vanilla bean, scraping the seeds into the milk, then drop in the pot. Heat to a simmer, remove from heat, cover, and set to infuse 10 minutes.

In bowl using an electric mixer, beat the yolks with the sugar until pale. Beat in the flour. Pull the vanilla bean from the milk and whisk the milk gradually into the egg mixture. Pour back into the saucepan, bring to a boil, and cook 1 minute. Remove from the heat and stir in the framboise. Strain into a bowl, cover with plastic wrap, and set aside to cool. When chilled, whip the cream and gently fold it in.

Spread the pastry cream evenly in the base of the prepared cookie crust. Arrange the berries neatly over top.

LAMINGTONS WITH JAM AND VANILLA CREAM AND CHOCOLATE ICING

TOTAL TIME: 3hrs 30min
Prep: 3hrs 30min
Cook: 40 min
YIELD: 15 servings
LEVEL: Capable cook

EQUIPMENT
20 x 30cm slice pan, piping bag, and 1cm star nozzle

INGREDIENTS
- 250g butter
- 215g (1 cup) caster sugar
- 3 eggs
- 2 teaspoons vanilla extract
- 300g (2 cups) self-raising flour
- 125ml (1/2 cup) milk
- 170g (2 cups) desiccated coconut
- 300ml thickened cream
- 1/2 teaspoon vanilla bean paste
- 245g (3/4 cup) strawberry jam

CHOCOLATE COATING
- 450g (3 cups) icing sugar mixture
- 2 tablespoons dark Dutch cocoa
- 30g butter, chopped
- 185ml (3/4 cup) water, boiling

DIRECTIONS

1. Preheat oven to 180C/160C fan forced. Line base and sides of a 20 x 30cm slice pan with baking paper. Use electric beaters to beat butter and sugar in a bowl until pale and creamy. Beat in eggs well, 1 at a time.
2. Beat in extract. Fold in flour and milk until well combined. Pour into prepared pan. Smooth. Bake for 35-40 minutes or until a skewer comes out clean. Cool in pan for 10 minutes. Transfer to a wire rack to cool.
3. Trim cake edges. Cut into 15 squares. Set a wire rack over a tray. Place coconut on a plate. For coating, place icing sugar, cocoa and butter in a heatproof bowl. Pour over boiling water. Stir until melted and combined.
4. Place a cake square in choc coating. Use 2 forks to turn to coat. Remove and allow excess coating to drain off. Roll in coconut to coat. Place on wire rack for 30 minutes to set. Repeat with remaining cake squares, cocoa mixture and coconut.
5. Use electric beaters with a whisk attachment to whisk cream and vanilla bean paste in a bowl until firm peaks form. Spoon into a piping bag fitted with a 1cm star nozzle. Use a serrated knife to cut the lamingtons horizontally (see Tip 6, page 106).
6. Spread 2 tsp of jam on 1 cut side of lamington. Pipe cream on top. Top with remaining lamington half. Place carefully on a tray. Repeat with remaining lamingtons, jam and cream. Place tray in the fridge for 30 minutes, to set the cream.

GLOSSARY OF AUSTRALIAN SLANG

Strike a light – an exclamation of surprise or frustration.
Back of Bourke – a very long way away.
In a Jiff – in a minute, very soon.
Vaca – pronounced vay-kay - vacation, holiday.
Stellar – outstanding.
Senior Sergeant – ranking officer in the Australian police force.
Roos – Kangaroos
Keen – very interested/interesting.
Real Crank – a crazy person.
Favs – favourites.
A few clicks – a few kilometres(miles).
Mobile phone – cell phone.
Strewth – exclamation, mild oath.
Nipper – child.
Right as rain – satisfactory, comfortable, well.
Bonza – most excellent, cool, great etc.
Spiffy – great, excellent.
Fair dinkum – true, genuine.
Dipstick – a loser, idiot.
Fossick – search, rummage.
Good oil – useful information, a good idea, the truth.
Old biddy – old woman.
Bloke – man.
Noggin – head.
Too right – definitely.
Got crook – was ill.
A goner – person or thing that is dead, lost, or past recovery or rescue.
Drongo – idiot.
Down in the dumps – sad, unhappy.

Pav - Pavlova – a dessert consisting of a meringue base or shell filled with whipped cream and fruit.
The Sarge – nickname for Sergeant.
Brekkie – breakfast.
Spit the Dummy – a sudden display of anger or frustration; to lose one's temper.
Give you a ring – call on the telephone.
Back of beyond – a remote place.
Delish – delicious.
Deadset – true, the truth.
Fella – man.
Pull the wool over someone's eyes – to deceive someone.
Bugger – used as a term of abuse, especially for a man or used to express annoyance or anger.
Bunyip – the bunyip, or kianpraty, is a large mythical creature from Aboriginal mythology, said to lurk in swamps, billabongs, creeks, riverbeds, and waterholes.
Drop bear – a dropbear or drop bear is a fictitious Australian marsupial.
To string along – to keep someone waiting or in a state of uncertainty.
Bonkers – crazy.
Sheila – a woman.
Ratbag – trouble maker or someone causing havoc.
Bugger off – go away, leave a person alone.
Bludger – an idle or lazy person.
Donkey Track – very rough, unpaved road.
Chuck a wobbly – to overreact to something.
Flat out like a lizard drinking – very busy.
Give it a burl – give something a go. To have a try at something.
Give them the flick – to break up with somebody.

Had a gutful – fed up, had enough.
Have tickets on oneself – to have a high opinion of oneself.
Mad as a cut snake – furious.
She'll be right – it will all be okay.

DON'T MISS ANOTHER BOOK BY K.J. EMRICK!

Subscribe to http://www.kathrineemrick.com/cozyregistration.html to be notified when the next books in the Pine Lake Inn, Darcy Sweet Mysteries or other books by K.J. Emrick are available.

I promise not to spam you or chit-chat too much, and only make occasional book release announcements.

Once you are registered you will be notified of new releases as they become available. Also from time to time I will give away a free story or other free gifts and have competitions for the people on my notification list, so keep a look out for those.:)

ABOUT THE AUTHOR

Strongly influenced by authors like James Patterson, Dick Francis, and Nora Roberts, Kathrine Emrick is an up and coming talent in the writing world. She is a Kindle author/publisher and brings a variety of experiences and observations to her writing.

Based in Australia, Kathrine has wanted to be an author for the majority of her life and can always be found jotting down daily notes in a journal. Like many authors, she loves to be surrounded by books and is a voracious reader.

In her spare time, she enjoys spending time with her family and volunteering at the local library.

Her goal is to become a bestselling author, regularly producing noteworthy content and engaging in a community of readers and writers.

To find out more please visit the Kathrine's website at kathrineemrick.com.

Printed in Great Britain
by Amazon